Venatores Noctis: Chronicles of a Royal Hunting Family

Albert Oon

ISBN: 9798815244597

SHORT STORIES WITH EXTRAS

Redraw of the original cover by @An_dres_art (on Twitter)

The new cover for this story by Albert Oon before it was replaced by @An_dres_art's cover.

The original cover for this story by Albert Oon before it

became the first story in the Venatores Noctis series.

Chapter 1 – Immortal but Dead

The last thing that Raven Aurora remembers was that he was having a hard time resisting the temptations of demons after coming home from ridding a group of demon worshippers that set themselves up in the town that he helped protect. He told his family that he was tired, needed his rest and that he loved them. He then prayed a rosary to silence his temptations before falling asleep. Now, he's found himself in what looks to be a ceremonial room with skeletons littering the floor. Unintelligible images of what happened flash in Raven's mind as he stands up only to stumble and fall into the skeletons. He quickly backs away as he sees the sharp teeth in many of the mouths of the skeletons.

"What are these people? Where am I and what happened here?" he asks himself.

Venatores Noctis: Chronicles of a Royal Hunting Family

Looking around, Raven finds a sword with complex

engravings on it that include designs of crosses, snakes, and

lions.

"A sword made for royalty, huh? I knew there was

corruption within them, but didn't know it was this bad,"

Raven says as his eyes unintentionally focus on his

reflection in the sword.

Since it is dark in the room, he can't make out his

own appearance. He sees something disgusting in it that

looks similar to a corpse; however, he assumes it's just his

eyes imagining things so he gets up and walks up the stairs

and out of the room to see that he's in a decrepit castle on a

mansion that overlooks the town he lives in. The moonlight

strangely fills Raven with energy and the grungy tired

feeling that he had that was like waking up after being

beaten in a fight is gone. Seeing as how he has enough light

to see his reflection in the sword, he does so and is

horrified to see that his face is rotting with half of it already off. In addition, his hair and skin are completely snow white, his eyes are as black as the night, and his mouth contains four sharp teeth like those of a beast.

"No, this can't be!" he says in denial.

Raven searches the house for a real mirror and finds one near the main entrance of the mansion to confirm what he knows to be real. This larger mirror gives him a better picture of himself that he smashes in frustration.

"Whoever did this to me will pay!" he says as he leaves the mansion.

To his surprise, Raven runs through the forest like a horse charging into battle and can leap into the air and climb through the trees like an aggressive primate. In the dark forest, he hears the cries of distress and quickly goes to it and finds a young family being assaulted by two people who have the same fangs that Raven has and what looks to be a wolf that can stand on its two legs. He jumps into action with his sword drawn so that no further harm can come to the family.

"Stop right there, you beasts!" Raven says.

The fanged people look at him and are full of mixed emotions but chose to laugh first.

"You call us beasts? Haha! You're a vampire just like us!" one of them says.

"Vampires? I demand that you tell me what those are."

"I'd call it funny that you don't know, but it does make sense since you were asleep for five years in that mansion on the cliff."

"Five years?"

"We'd waken you up earlier if your guardian angel wasn't protecting you from us. I must thank you for bringing yourself to us," another mentions.

"What for? What did you need me for? What did you do to me?"

"We wanted to make the first vampire someone who could make the world despair and what better person than you who is a well known hero? Unfortunately, God had other plans and messed it all up through your guardian angel, but it looks like the sacrament to make you into a vampire was successful. It seems that He has abandoned you."

"I'm still here despite your curse, so that's obviously not true."

"But it's the curse and how you became a vampire that proves His abandonment. You see, a person becomes a vampire through a blasphemous sacrament that involves a ritual where the main ingredients require a baptized infant. We took your newly born son, cut his throat, tore out his still beating heart, and poured his blood all over you while you were under our influence."

"No, that can't be!" Raven says.

Clearer flashes from before come into his mind to confirm that what this vampire is saying is correct.

"Oh, but it is! We've even killed other members of your family to drench you in their blood and create other vampires. It's a shame that their sacrifice was mostly in vain."

"I'll kill you for this!"

Raven strikes one of the vampires with his sword only for it to break when it hits them causing no pain and for both to laugh.

"Haha! Only holy weapons can kill a vampire and there's nothing about you that's holy! You have no choice but to join our side and fight against the God who let us control you and turn you into what you are."

Again, yelling out in anger, Raven uses his fists and this allows him to punch a hole through a vampire's chest. Everyone is shocked by this except for Raven who still has his faith in God.

"So much for nothing about me being holy," Raven says.

"This changes nothing! No wait, it does! I get to say that I killed the hero Raven by myself! Serf, come to my aid!"

The wolf quickly leaps at Raven who is then killed even quicker as Raven raises his leg and brings it down in the blink of an eye to crush the oncoming wolf's skull into bits. This display of strength forces the other vampire to act against its fear and stab Raven in the neck with its serrated dagger, however, this has no effect. Raven then grabs the vampire's arm and crushes it with a single hand before using his other hand to lift the screaming vampire in the air and crushing its neck until its head falls off. Even after venting his anger on these unholy creatures, Raven is filled with agony, sadness, and anger, so he lets out a yell before uncontrollably sobbing for his family.

This along with his other actions has scared the family that he was trying to protect, but the daughter of the family starts to become sympathetic to him because of the honesty of his sadness. She approaches him to her parent's dismay with her hand out to help him.

"Mr. Aurora, thank you for helping us. What can we do to repay you?" the young girl asks.

Raven pulls himself together for the girl then says, "Just-just be safe when I bring you back to town. I'll handle the rest from there."

"There…there is no place safe in the world."

"What are you talking about?"

"The vampires and their slaves are everywhere. There's no place in the world that's safe to be."

"Then I'll just have to stain the entire world with their blood."

"Is that even possible?"

"I can still live despite being a walking corpse and having a knife jabbed in my neck," Raven says while effortlessly taking out the vampire's knife and tossing it aside as if it were nothing, "I think it's possible and by God's grace, I will defeat the vampires. If you say they are everywhere, I'll start by cleaning up my hometown and restoring everyone's faith. That'll at least make one place in the world safe. Stay close behind me, but not too close. This is going to get messy."

Chapter 2 – Weapon of Faith

Various vampire rulers of the town known as Horizon talk about their plans for the people they hold people over. This meeting takes place in what was once the grand cathedral of the town and the meeting is more like a dinner rather than a strictly business meeting as the vampires indulge in the blood of their serfs and the finest meals that their serf chefs can make. The most business that gets done during the meeting is the exchange of serfs and inflating of pride.

"Here is the most beautiful woman on earth," one says.

"Here is the most handsome and hardworking boy in the land!" another says.

Men, women, and children of all ages, and body types do their dance and parade themselves around the table in outfits that show more than hide.

"Look what I did to this man who once called himself the Spear of His Home. Now, he's truly a watchdog," a vampire says while pointing to the half-man, half-dog person in the room.

"Look what I did to this bishop. His appearance matches his snake behavior," another says.

"Look, my serfs are other vampire lords that I beat in a sword fight."

"Look at my genius through the beauty of mine."

"Yours is nothing more than an amalgamation of different animals and human body parts."

"That's what's so beautiful and special about it. Despite its many parts that don't seem like they should fit, it lives anyway and can do a myriad of tasks even the more perverse one should you require it."

"No thank you. I have plenty of livestock for that purpose."

It is then that Raven crashes his way into the room much to everyone's surprise. Everyone turns to look at him except for the serfs and vampires who are too dazed from their drugs and drinking to do anything.

"I'm sorry. Did I interrupt anything important?" Raven says while looking around, "I see that some of you that I trusted have broken that trust for temporary gains."

"These gains aren't temporary. They are eternal," a vampire who was once a cardinal says.

"Drink of the blood of these slaves and you'll have your youthful appearance restored to you," another familiar face says.

"I don't want to hear anything out of a charity worker who now dines on the people he served," Raven retorts.

"Charity only pays so much. The devils have given us immortality on earth. It's a far better gift than immortality in Heaven. At least we don't need to toil and uselessly suffer day in and out for an uncaring God."

Raven puts his fist through the vampire's face then says, "Cease your blasphemy!"

The rest of the vampires take out their weapons and have their serfs ready to defend them.

"Think carefully about your next decision, Raven. The only reason we aren't killing you now is because we didn't like that trash you killed. You'll be making dangerous enemies if you do not embrace the vampire within you."

"I'd rather not ally myself with traitorous clergy, royals, and peasants."

"Do you not yet realize how outnumbered you are? You don't even have a weapon."

"You are mistaken. I am the weapon."

After saying this, Raven leaps up then kills the cardinal he once knew. The rest of the vampires and their serfs descend upon him but can't do much of any damage to him. Because of this, his new heightened reactions, and combat prowess, Raven comes out of the fight with his clothes and armor being the only things that get damaged. The lesser vampires, their serfs, and the other civilians of Horizon gather around the cathedral and watch as Raven walks out covered in the blood of his enemies.

"Who wishes to share the fate of the damned that I have killed? Who can kill who is already dead such as I? Present yourselves as my challenger or run to your wretched lords and tell them that God's will shall no longer be ignored!" Raven states.

The cowardly vampires and some of their serfs run away from the town as the light of faith is restored in it. On the other hand, the civilians and some of the serfs bow down and praise God for this blessing. Raven then proceeds to help clean his hometown. The first thing that he does is take off the bodies of those who opposed the vampires and their serfs. Some of these bodies are people he recognizes such as bishops, princes, princesses, nuns, farmers, and other simple folk and neighbors he used to exchange smiles and gifts with. Another familiar face hears of his sudden appearance and races to see him.

"Raven!" he says as he runs to him.

"Confessor Rinaldo!" Raven says as he goes to meet the priest halfway.

Rinaldo doesn't mind that he is hugging his rotting friend. He is only glad to see him again. Raven is much the same way and is happy to see a familiar face after seeing the dead bodies of so many of his friends and family.

"I've missed you so much, brother."

"I've missed you too. I'm sorry you have to see me this way."

"It doesn't bother me. In fact, I'm glad that you're here and that you can defeat the vampires with your bare hands."

"Can you do it as well? You're a weapon of God like I am."

"I'm afraid that I have to rely on my holy water, sword, and shield if I want to fight them face to face. I still have yours if you need them. You seem invincible as you are."

"Hmm. I could use my family's whip."

"Ah, yes, but that was sent to Rome along with your second youngest son."

"He's alive?!"

"Yes, we sent him there so that he can learn how to be a soldier like how we trained."

Raven falls to his knees and crosses himself.

"Thanks be to God that I have at least one child that's still alive!"

He then begins to sob tears of joy before collecting himself and standing back up.

"The rest of your family is dead?"

"Yes, the vampires took them and sacrificed them in their blasphemous sacraments as they made me and their own into vampires. I was under their influence the entire time and couldn't do anything to save them. It's a good thing that the damned fools died soon after."

"It is indeed, but still a tragedy. The devil worshippers must've put some kind of spell on you after you cleared their hideout. We all knew something was strange with you especially since you took your family away from the town and left without your second youngest. God must have great plans for that boy."

Venatores Noctis: Chronicles of a Royal Hunting Family

"I still feel unworthy to be alive. I fell to the influence of demons and devil worshippers even after all my prayers and trying to serve God as best I can. There must've been something wrong I've done to deserve this. Was I blind to my sins or did I blind myself to it? Perhaps it was a generational demon that's cursed my family or-"

"Stop it with this useless reflection. You brought honor to your dishonorable family's name and you came back just when your home needed you most. Even the just Job fell to tragedy even though he was a blameless man."

The people around the two who hear what they're talking about recount to Raven his actions. Of his heroics in saving the town from bandits and devil worshippers to simpler things like giving gifts and simple advice to them when they needed it.

"Thank you, everyone. There's nothing I can do to repay this kindness other than to seek the reason why God allowed me to become a vampire."

"We'll discover it together and I think I know where we can start. There's a hidden clan of vampires known as the Corpus that are said to be repentant of their sins. Many including the vampires think that they are just myths because of how a person becomes a vampire and slave to their sin, but because of you, I think they truly exist. We should seek them out and ask them what you should do. We could also visit your son in Rome if you'd like."

"I think it'd be better if I visit the Corpus first. I'd rather not have my son see me this way."

"I understand."

A citizen comes running to the two as they say, "Sir knights! The vampires are sending their serfs at us!"

"Their testing our faith again so soon. They either have a clever plan, being fools, or too cowardly to admit that they lost this town."

"It's probably the last two."

"I assume this as well. Regardless of this, let's get to where they are to meet them with force."

At the gates of Horizon, many guards stand with their weapons drawn and ready for battle. Archers have their ballistas and bows armed and ready and the knights have their swords, maces, and axes blessed with holy water. In the distance, the vampires from before have gathered some of their nearby allies and sent their serf army ahead of them or rather to fight and die in their place. The archers send a rain of arrows on the serfs and the knights at the gates defeat those that remain. This quick victory is due to the restored faith of the civilians in Horizon that have strengthened the weapons of the soldiers and lessened the power of evil in the area. The vampires retreat with their horses and hope that their superiors do not punish them too severely.

"That was fast. We didn't even need to act," Raven says as the people celebrate their second victory in the row.

"That's the power of faith, my brother. I've also trained each of these men and women personally," Rinaldo says.

"Of course. It's good to know that my home will be safe without my help."

"It'll be safe without our help since I'm going with you to find the Corpus."

"Are you sure they'll be okay without your help?"

"You've seen it yourself."

"Fine then. It'll be good to fight alongside you again."

"It'll be like the good old days, but at least we don't need to have any pity for the damned."

"Will you be able to keep up with me? You already had a hard time keeping up with me in terms of combat prowess."

"That's because I was doing confessions and blessing the dead during battle. Do not worry about me

Venatores Noctis: Chronicles of a Royal Hunting Family

because I have with me the whip of St. Peter Damian. It's not the same whip that whipped Christ Himself that your family has, but the blessings that it has have saved me and others more than once."

"I believe you. Let us head off then. I am eager to learn my God-given purpose."

The two say their farewells to the people of Horizon before heading off by horse to a location in the mountains where the Corpus are rumored to be. Meanwhile, the vampires that had control over and attacked Horizon tell their lords of their defeat. A few are taken away to be tortured while the lords think about what to do, but at the same time, are not too worried since most of the world is still theirs.

Chapter 3 – Hunting the Dead

Two vampires and their serfs pick over the remains of a small settlement that most except for the few people that live near it know about.

"You thought you could escape without paying your just dues to us You thought wrong," one vampire says.

They decapitate their prey and make the heads of their prey into necklaces that they put around their necks and the necks of their serfs as if they were medals of honor

Venatores Noctis: Chronicles of a Royal Hunting Family

and use the leftover body parts as decorations and warnings

to those who chose to act like these people. The sound of

horses coming to the town stops the vampires and their

serfs from doing anything else as they eagerly await more

prey, however, they are disappointed to see two horses

without their riders entering the town. Being distracted by

the horses costs them their lives as Rinaldo and Raven kill

them from behind.

"The allure of prey is too much for them to resist.

This is also the fate of faithless places and the places that

are losing faith in God," Rinaldo says.

"Is the Church's army still the largest and strongest

in the land?" Raven asks.

"The vampires wouldn't be in control if it was. In

fact, the Church's army can only defend Rome, their supply

convoys, and their small scale attacks on vampire

controlled towns, and force isn't the vampires' primary

way of taking over. It's through their influence. This is why they were able to take over most of the world in five years."

"Then to get rid of them all will take multiple faithful generations, which sounds impossible."

"That seems to be so."

"Perhaps, this is why you've been given the temporary immortality of a vampire. Maybe you're going to be the leader of these future generations. You were a great father after all."

"'Were' is the keyword there. I still feel guilty for not being able to save my family."

"You have your son, me, and the other members of the Church to look after. There are still people on this earth who are worth protecting."

"You're right."

"We should go. It doesn't look like there's anyone left here that would know about the Corpus."

Rinaldo and Raven leave the ruined town and make their way to another one. This one appears to be abandoned with signs that people are definitely here.

"Hello!" Raven calls out, "Is anyone here? You have nothing to be afraid of. We are holy men and I am not your typical vampire."

"And we are not your typical villagers. Leave now. This village is cursed by the vampires," a voice says from the dark.

"Let us help you then. In return, we only ask for information to find the Corpus."

Men with the bodies of snakes, apes, wolves, other animals step out of the dark. Other men and women step out as well. These more normal looking people have the crests of their former vampire masters on them and scars of abuse and experimentation.

"You people are serfs?" Rinaldo asks.

"We are no longer serfs. We either managed to escape our slavers or managed to survive them throwing us away and ending up here. We aren't welcome anywhere else because of our past."

"You can go to Horizon. Serfs are welcome there as long as you are repentant."

"Horizon? That city is under the control of powerful vampire lords."

"It was but we freed it. Now it is a sanctuary for the faithful including serfs like you. Tell them that Rinaldo and Raven sent you for extra insurance if you don't think they'll accept you."

"Raven and Rinaldo. Ah, I see. I knew you too looked familiar. You two are also the talk of the local vampires who are planning to take your heads to gain more wealth and power than they already have. You best leave this area for your own safety."

"That's not going to happen. You said that this place is cursed and I plan to help you purify it," Raven says.

"I was speaking figuratively. We are cursed with these appearances and the area has a few resting checkpoints for the vampires that force us to hide while they pillage the surrounding area and our homes if they come across here."

"Resting checkpoints?"

"The vampires sustain themselves with sin because their rotten souls are slaves to it. In addition, if they go too long without blood, their skin begins to rot and fall off their bodies. This is why they have many checkpoints across the land where they can indulge in whatever sin they find themselves unable to resist. I said they are pitiable creatures if they weren't the reason for their soul's enslavement."

"We'll eliminate whatever checkpoints they have and draw their attention to us so you can live in peace here or join Horizon. In exchange, we only ask for more information about the Corpus."

"That sounds like a fair trade, but are you sure you can handle such large numbers one after the other? The Corpus are rumored to be able to handle entire bands of vampires singlehandedly and win without even being fazed by being injured. I say rumored because I've never seen one in battle.

"We can handle it, but if you want to join, you're free to join the assault."

"Hmm. We'll consider it after watching your abilities in battle."

"That's fair. Let's show them what the knights of the Church can do, Rinaldo."

After being told by the serfs the locations of the checkpoints, Rinaldo and Raven scout them out before attacking. The checkpoints are more lavish than they originally thought. These spots are mini-vacation spots as well as a place where the vampires can partake in the blasphemous sacraments. Here women who are forced to bear children for the vampire's baptism are raped by serfs since vampires aren't able to conceive children and priests are forced to baptize the infants for the sacrifice. The children that grow up before they can be sacrificed are either turned into serfs, become sacrifices for a different sacrament, or turned into blood slaves for the vampire's nourishment.

Seeing this alone sets off something in Raven causing him to immediately attack the vampires and their serfs and tear them to shreds. Rinaldo only manages to pick off those who are fleeing the fight since most of the attention is on Raven who has no problem fighting on his own. Soon, the checkpoint is empty of sinners and freed of its slaves.

"You work as fast as always," Rinaldo says.

"I have a purpose and my targets. There's nothing more than a reaper of the Lord needs to know," Raven says.

"Reaper of the Lord? I'm surprised you remember that title we had for our squad."

"I remember more of my life than I expect. Perhaps, it's a benefit or curse of being dead. I remember every happy memory and sin that I've committed as if it all happened yesterday. Anyways, we should get rid of the next checkpoint. Knowing what is happening in them is making my blood boil like a sinner in the depths of Hell."

The two head to the next checkpoint and scout it out again before attacking, but while scouting, Raven overhears the slaves how they love this life of pleasure and slavery. What especially gets Raven mad is the women that don't mind being used as baby factories nor do the men mind being used by both the female and male vampires as long as they get paid in pleasure and money. This pushes Raven into action as he begins to kill not only the vampires and their serfs but also the willing slaves who have subjected themselves to evil. He even kills a pregnant woman by slamming the face of one man into hers so both are crushed into the ground together. Seeing this in the distance, Rinaldo quickly ends his fight so he can run over to the woman and cuts open her pregnant belly to find that the baby is miraculously alive.

"What's wrong with you? Do you not realize that some of these women are still pregnant?" Rinaldo says.

"I...I...can't control..." Raven struggles to say as he is still shaking from his anger.

Several serfs that have feigned repentance ambush the two with their dead masters' weapons, which forces Rinaldo and Raven to fight back.

"Why arc you doing this? Your masters are dead and you are free!" Rinaldo asks.

"They gave us the life we wanted! They gave us riches and pleasures beyond our imagination while God only gave us pain and misery! I'll kill you for killing them and find another master to serve!" the delusional serf responds.

Rinaldo is then forced to either kill the serfs who refuse to be taken prisoner or run away. Raven has no problem killing the serfs even the pregnant women. Again, Rinaldo tries to save the infants and finds that he is unable to save some of them and has to baptize the dead ones to save their souls from Limbo.

"Raven! Have you lost your sense?" Rinaldo says.

"I…I don't feel like I'm always in control of myself," Raven admits before saying, "Why should I have mercy on this scum anyway? The infants will go to Limbo then Heaven anyway if they die, which is a fate better than living in this vampire infested world."

"You should know that you should still give them a chance at life. God only knows what purpose He has for them. Why are you even saying these things? I know you know to do better than this."

"I'm sorry. I…I don't know."

"He's a vampire. He doesn't have any control of his actions," one of the repentant serfs that Raven and Rinaldo are helping says as they come in, "Or at least that's what the Corpus told us."

"We haven't cleared out all the checkpoints around your home yet. You don't need to reward us with information about them yet," Rinaldo says.

"You have done enough to show us your conviction. Raven, the Corpus that we've met had the same problems that you have. Currently, they reside in a cave in the largest mountain in this region, which is not too far from where you met us. The only conclusion they came to about their condition was that they were dead and they were subject to the current state of their soul and the will of God. Concern yourself solely with finding them and your purpose afterward if you can. As for us beastmen and sinners, we will do our penance by bringing the infants, repentant serfs, and slaves you saved to Horizon and helping where we can there. Farewell, knights of the Church."

The beastmen and serfs head off in the direction of Horizon as Raven heads in the direction of the Corpus.

"Wait," Rinaldo says.

"What? I want to find out the reason why I'm like this and I can't stop myself from moving forward. Please, Rinaldo, you must believe me," Raven says.

"I guess it makes sense that you can't control yourself like how the other vampires can't help but indulge in sin and you're still my brother, so I'll believe you. Let's confirm this truth with the Corpus and find out what the Lord has in store for you."

"Thank you, brother."

Venatores Noctis: Chronicles of a Royal Hunting Family

Rinaldo and Raven take their horses to the

mountains while spies for the vampires head back with this

information for their masters in the hopes that something

will be done about them.

Chapter 4 – Sacrifices from the Dead for the Living

The spies of the vampires report to their lords the news of what happened because of Rinaldo and Raven.

"Who cares about those rumored Corpus! All they do is sulk in the shadows and do their penance. They are bound by God and rarely if ever pose a problem for us, which is our sign of victory. God has abandoned this world and given it to us just as the demons have told us," a vampire lord says.

"Still, we must give them the bodies they desire. We have enough corpses for them to start bringing their army over," another says.

"Why rush our complete takeover of the earth? Savor the desperation of the humans because when they're gone, we'll only have ourselves to fight over," yet another lord points out.

"If it's desperation you want, perhaps we should bring a single demon over or maybe multiple demons in a single body. That will cause absolute despair in the hearts of those cowards in Rome and be more for the Corpus to handle."

"Oh, dear, you know better than to tempt me with that, but because I'm so curious, let's try it out. Prepare the ritual and the corpses for the ceremony."

While this is happening, Rinaldo and Raven enter a large cave big enough for their horses and themselves to enter with enough room to fit wagons for supplies to go in and out, and the wheel marks in the dirt show that wagons, horses, and people have gone in and out of the cave. There are no torches or sources of light in the cave, which forces Rinaldo to light a torch as they continue further deeper into the mountain. The sound of stones moving and footsteps put the two on high alert as they look around for the source of the noise.

"Hello? We mean you no harm. I am like you in search of answers to my God-given purpose," Raven says.

"Ha! Harm. If you could harm or even end our lives, that would be a grace. If you are like us, then you are not in search of anything and are instead directed here like how your horse was directed to this mountain," a hissing voice says from the dark.

"Then help me understand. I'm begging you!"

Dark figures approach the two from the darkness. Raven thinks these figures are cloaked in shadow, however, on closer inspection, it is revealed that these figures are

Venatores Noctis: Chronicles of a Royal Hunting Family

actually pitched black. They are like a walking skeleton

with the teeth of a vampire, very few bits of flesh left on

them, and a hollow center and eyes. Both Raven and

Rinaldo are a bit startled by their appearance, but the horses

are not because of their holy presence. Many of them look

the same with small differences in their bodies in faces

though all look eerie to an ordinary person.

"So, you want to learn?" one of them says.

"Yes," Raven answers.

"Wrong. You are being given the grace of this

information through us who are simple mouthpieces.

Follow us as this truth is told."

On cue, Raven follows the Corpus further into the

cave with Rinaldo following from behind.

The Corpus continues, "You want to know the

answer to an obvious question. When we are alive, it is

through grace that we are able to change for the better and,

through sin, our behavior decays. When we are dead, the

state of our souls is frozen in place for God to judge and nothing can change it, but just like the souls in Purgatory, we are only perfected if we reach Heaven. This is why you still may commit the same evil deeds you did when you were alive, however, you will not be held accountable for them since you have no control over yourself and because you are already dead."

"My brother, Raven, is no unrepentant sinner," Rinaldo points out.

"I have sinned many times in my life and many of the times that I confessed, I confessed to a different confessor so that you would not hear my shameful acts," Raven admits without really wanting to, "Even though we prayed for our enemies before battle and fought for justice, I did feel lost in the slaughter every now and then."

"That would explain your loss in control, but your virtue should've outshined your vices. Why would God resign you and these Corpus to the fate of a vampire?"

"It is something God only knows and God has resigned most of us to a fate of penance in the dark as you can see," a Corpus says as they reach the inner chamber of the mountain.

Though Rinaldo cannot see very well, he can see hundreds of Corpus in the area all of which have the same eerie appearance.

"Here, we all starve both for food and for a purpose. We all came here against our will and yet not against our soul's natural inclination to follow the Divine Will's command," the Corpus continues, "Some of us were no different from the vampires outside. I was once a lord who commanded many armies until the grace within my soul caused me to repentant and embrace an eternity of penance. Some of us even leave this cave to do the same things we did in life only to come back much like how we sinned and eventually came back to God over and over again."

"Is there no end to this penance?" Raven asks.

"If God so wills it. There are some who simply fade into the dust after a period of time or leave the cave to do some deed then never return and share the same fate as the first that I mentioned. Still, we do not know if all of us will enter Heaven, but that could just be the despair that I struggled with talking. Perhaps we all will enter Heaven since our bodies are holy enough to fight the vampires hand to hand. Even still, we have few to no one who prays for us unlike the souls in Purgatory, so our pain is all the more amplified by the length of this fate."

"Isn't this a bit much even for you whose bodies follow the will of God?" Rinaldo asks.

"The price paid for each of us to be vampires is the death of an innocent infant and the price paid for our redemption was that of innocence and truth itself on the cross. Even one sin is one sin too many. The cost of a single sin is too steep, too expensive for any of us to pay, and yet, we've acted like the price was worth it. We trade our souls for the vanities of life and in the end, come out with less than what we had because of it."

"Enough of your sulking. If you want to be freed from your penance, then pay the price to the last penny. I'm here to find what God wills of me to do," Raven states.

Many of the Corpus look at him because of what he said.

"If you are knights, then you are probably here to fight with us in a very particular battle. One that may finally give the vampires control over the world if they win it."

"If they win? We are invincible against them. How can we not win?"

"Remember that we are completely subject to God's will and if God wills that the vampires win, then they will win."

"What is this battle fought over anyway?"

"The vampires are giving a legion of demons a single body made of an uncountable number of human sacrifices. If the demons obtain that body, then many more will despair and fall into the hands of demons while the few remaining become lifelong slaves."

"Then what are we waiting for? Let's head out to where this is taking place so we can put a stop to it."

"Again, we move when the will of God moves us, and right now, it appears that you were the one we were waiting for," a Corpus interrupts as a large portion of them gather around Raven.

"I haven't done anything but starve and pray for years despite wanting to do something, and now, I feel like I have the strength of a hundred men. I am ready to fight," another Corpus says.

Many more say similar things in how they are ready to fight the vampires after being inactive for so long.

Raven gets off his horse then says, "Thank you for showing me my purpose. Together, we will do this great deed for our penance to save not only ourselves from the pains of our sins but also the world."

The Corpus cheer and quickly clear out of the mountain at lightning fast speeds as they finally have something that will pay for a majority if not all their penance.

Raven is about to join them until Rinaldo calls to him and says, "Wait for me! I must join you in this battle, brother!"

"This is our penance to do. If you want to join, then try to keep up," Raven says before quickly catching up with the rest of the Corpus.

They exit the caves of the mountain and go through the forest moved by the will of God in the direction of their target. By the time they reach it, it is almost time for the sun to rise, however, instead of the sun being on the horizon, there is only a black sphere that gives off an uncomfortable warmth to the mortals who see it. The humans who look at the black sphere become tempted with a multitude of demons and the typical ways of resisting their influence such as prayer, ignoring it, and renewing the trust of their soul in God's hands hardly works. On the other hand, the Corpus aren't tempted at all and briskly continue on their way to the huge castle where the legion of demons is being summoned at. This castle is an amalgamation of parts of churches and kingdoms the vampires conquered like how the lords decorate themselves with the flesh and bits of the kings, popes, generals, and more men and women of valor that they killed.

As the vampires start the ceremony, the Corpus give the guards outside no time to react to them as they assault the castle head on and from the sides. Raven leads the attack and wastes no time charging through the enemies as thoughts about the innocent people and his son who could be affected by the demon's arrival fill his mind. He soon arrives at the site where the demon is going to be summoned and finds that this area is covered in the corpses of a seemingly uncountable number of bodies and a portal made of black stones that have various carvings in it and flames spewing from it. The vampire lords sit in their thrones with their weapons drawn. One lord sits in a throne of gold, another of naked mortals, one in a throne made of flesh, and the final one being made of exotic kinds of food. There are other destroyed thrones near them some of which look to be in the process of being made.

"We expected either vampires or humans to come to stop us, but we didn't expect a corpse to come to us, and you least of all, Raven," a lord says.

"It's over, you wretched sinners. The Corpus and I will stop this ritual of yours and there's nothing you can do," Raven says.

"Speaking about that, the ritual is nearly complete so whatever you do is useless, and you call people like us vain. The one thing you can do is go through the portal into the Hell to shut it off from the other side. That is the only way to stop it. From what I've heard, you have no real control of yourself, and your soul is bound for Heaven, so will God abandon you and send you to Hell just to save the world? I'm curious to see how this plays out."

More Corpus enter the room in time to hear the way to stop the ritual. They look at each other and wonder what to do, especially Raven.

That is until Raven sets his heart on his goal then says, "Whatever happens, I submit all of my being to serving God. Even if I must enter Hell and stay there forever, I will do so if it means that God's will is done. I'm already dead after all."

The Corpus fight the vampire lords while Raven leaps into the portal. He feels in sync with the will of God

Venatores Noctis: Chronicles of a Royal Hunting Family

that moves him as he enters the fire. In Hell, Raven sees a

multitude of demons around the portal and many more

sinners burning in Hell below them. Not wanting to waste

time, he breaks the portal with his two hands. The demons

are about to attack him but are then stopped by a tornado of

flames that consume him. To his surprise, this tornado

transports Raven further into Hell until he appears in

Purgatory where his flesh burns away until only his soul

remains.

Now that his soul is purified, Raven enters into

Heaven and is happily reunited with his family and united

forever with the Heavenly family. The battle quickly ends

after this as the Corpus overwhelm the vampire lords with

might and sheer numbers. In the sky, the black sphere

disappears signaling the vampires' defeat. News of this

defeat quickly spread throughout the world and faith is

restored to many kingdoms as the vampires are fought back

to near extinction within a month. During this time,

Rinaldo teaches Raven's last son, Nevar, how to fight in appreciation for his brother and way to apologize for being late to the battle. Meanwhile, a small band of vampires plot their evil schemes in the dark, but as long as the light of faith and love of God shines in the hearts of men, sin will not rule the world.

The End

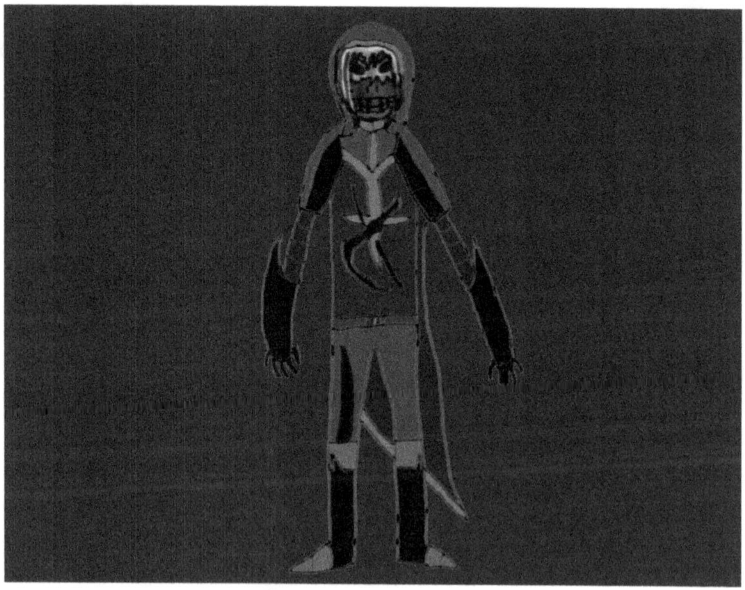

Concept art of Raven Aurora.

Raven Aurora redrawn by @An_dres_art.

Albert Oon

𝔅𝔢𝔥𝔦𝔫𝔡 𝔱𝔥𝔢 𝔖𝔱𝔬𝔯𝔶

- This series is heavily inspired by the *Castlevania* video game series by Konami.

- The main character is named Raven because I can reverse the name and come up with Nevar just like how Dracula's son is named Alucard, which is Dracula in reverse. My other idea was to call him Vlad, but Dalv doesn't sound that good of a name to me.

- Raven's appearance is inspired by Alucard's from *Castlevania: Symphony of the Night* and Leon from *Castlevania: Lament of Innocence.*

- Rinaldo is named after Rinaldo Gandolfi from *Castlevania.* I was going to name more characters after *Castlevania* characters, but thought it would be too lazy and on the nose.

- This story was originally going to be its own self-contained story bundled with more stories like it, however, because I was getting more ideas for stories in its setting, I decided to make it the starting point of the series. This decision to make it a series was also the main factor in leaving one of Raven's children alive for the sequel.

- The quote on the second cover that I came up with this for this story is from *I Have Seen Where It Grows* by Demon Hunter.

- I didn't expect @An_dres_art to redo the cover for this story since I only commissioned him to redo the character art for Raven. Because he did, I decided to use his version as the one shown on Smashwords and other distributors of the story so it wouldn't go to waste rather than keep the cross cover that is characteristic of this series.

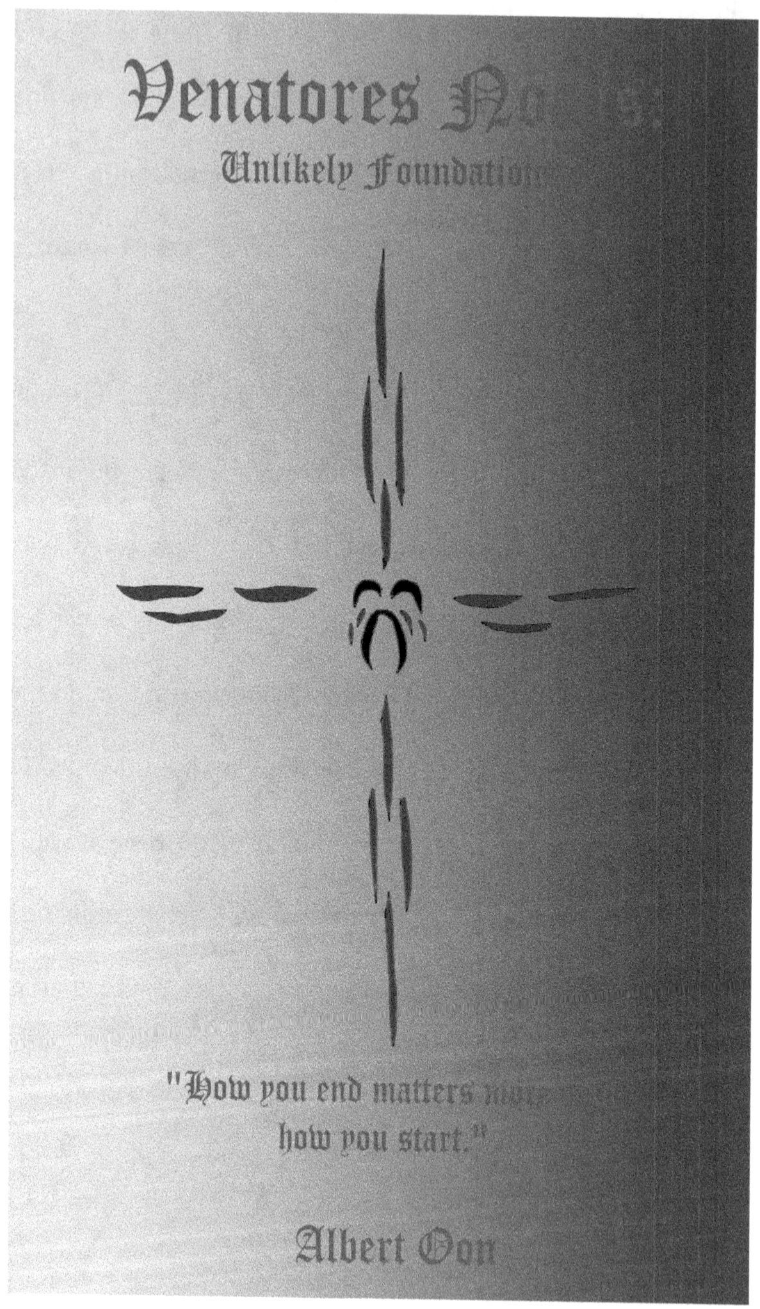
Venatores No...
Unlikely Foundatio...
"How you end matters m...
how you start."
Albert Oon

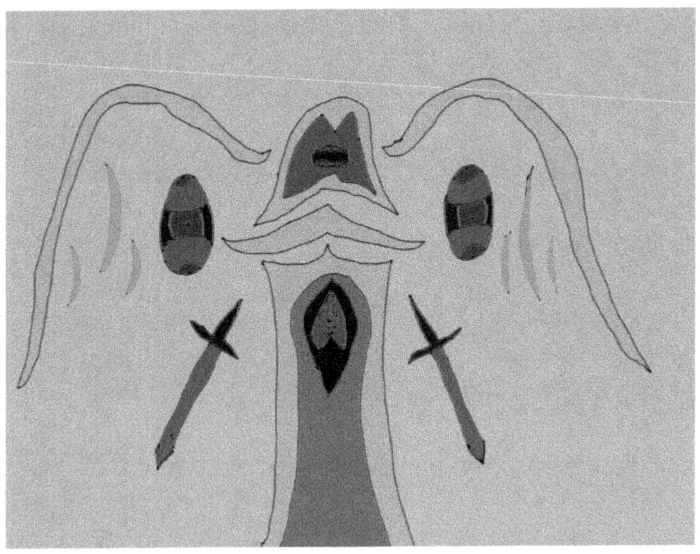

Chapter 1 – Pushed into Destiny

Nevar dreams about the day he lost his family a memory that haunts him to this very day. He was seven at the time and afraid of bringing home his bad test scores from school, so he wandered through the town until he realized that he would get in even more trouble if he came home late. By thc time he went home, he saw some strange people enter the house, which stopped him from going any further. He was always afraid of talking to weird looking strangers, but this time, his instincts were correct as these people hypnotize the rest of his family and exit the house with his family in tow. Despite wanting to do something, he was frozen in his fear and didn't go anywhere near his house until his family was far in the distance.

Turning to look at the house, he remembers the reports of what vampires do to their victims that they use in their blasphemous sacraments. He sees the broken, bloodied, and desecrated bodies of his family with his eyes focusing on the cut throat and torn out heart of his infant brother. Seeing this is enough to make him fall down in tears and not want to do anything about it.

"I'm useless. I couldn't do anything then and I can't do anything now to save those who are suffering the same fate," he says to himself.

"Stop being so hard on yourself," a familiar and comforting voice says to him.

Nevar looks up to see his father looking at him with a smile.

"Father…I'm not worthy to be called your son. I can't be the same hero you were," Nevar admits.

"You will be. I know it. Don't doubt yourself and remember to trust God to help you in everything you do," his father says.

"I do trust God. I trust Him more than myself."

"As you should. Do that and you will never fail."

Nevar feels himself beginning to wake up and he tries his best to will himself to stay in the dream.

"Wait, don't let me wake up, father! Tell me more! Grant me your intercession from your Heaven!"

"I will and I'll never leave you. You needn't worry so much. You are my son after all."

The young man calls out to his father again as he wakes up. Even though he is disappointed that he is awake, he puts aside his feelings to focus on his morning prayers. After his prayers and getting dressed, he takes his family's whip and heads out for training. Nevar passes by several others that are his age that are practicing with warrior priests and knights from the army teaching them. Many of his peers ignore him while others take note.

"Why bother coming out if you don't fight?" one of them says as they pass by him.

"I…I'm training to," Nevar answers.

"With the 'skill' that you've shown on our assignments, I'm surprised that you train at all."

The young knights walk away and leave Nevar to sulk in his embarrassment. That is until his teacher comes to him after overhearing the conversation.

"Do not worry about what they say. They only want you to be able to defend yourself. If not, then I expect to see them soon in the confessional," his teacher says.

"Uncle Rinaldo! I'm ready for today's training, sir," Nevar says as he follows his teacher to the training site.

"Are you? You look like you're letting what your peers said get to you."

"No, it's not that. At least not completely that. I saw my father in a dream and was reminded of him and what the vampires did to my family."

"Then you received a message from Heaven and your saintly father. I wish my brother would visit me in a dream sometime. What did he say?"

"He reminded me to trust in God, not to doubt myself, and that he'll never leave me."

"That's great! Why does this trouble you?"

"I wish the dream could've lasted longer so I could be with him longer and so he could give me more of his wisdom."

"Follow me and listen to what I have to say then if it is wisdom that you want. Today, we'll train outside the noise of the city and judging eyes of both your and my peers."

"Yes, uncle."

Nevar and Rinaldo go out to a homestead outside of the city. While looking at it from a distance, Nevar appreciates looking at it from the outside and the surrounding area.

"Beautiful even from a distance. You'll never find a city like Rome anywhere else in the world," Rinaldo says.

"Yes, she is though I can't say the same for sure since I've only been to one other city besides this one. Thank you for bringing me out here, uncle. Despite the city's loveliness, the change of scenery is refreshing," Nevar says.

"Your peers mock you for your combat ability and cowardice in battle. Prove that isn't true by fighting me with all your strength."

The two begin to fight and Nevar manages to fight on even ground even as Nevar uses a whip and Rinaldo uses a sword and shield.

"Good, good! Those friends of yours don't know what they're talking about," Rinaldo complements.

"They're not my friends nor do I fight the same way on assignments. Most of the time, I cower behind everyone and only come out when absolutely needed."

"That isn't so bad."

"What do you mean?"

"You come out when you're needed. What else can be asked of you?"

"I just want to do more like my father."

"What about like your uncle?"

"I'm sorry. I didn't mean to insult you, uncle."

"Haha, you didn't. Your father wanted to be lots of things and he was. He brought honor to your family when it had less than none by being an honorable knight of the Church. When we first met on the battlefield, I thought he was an arrogant man who wanted nothing more than glory and honor. Even after getting to know him better, he would always say that he was a better fighter, but it was through fighting with him, I saw the God loving man that he truly was."

"Are you saying I should be in the kind of battles that he was in?"

"No, not at all. Besides, our wars were fought against heathens and heretics rather than monsters. I'm just saying that you're like him in the way that you're there where you're needed even when others don't want you. When your father came back as a vampire, he was bothered by the fact that he came back in the way that he did and couldn't save your mother and siblings. In spite of that, he saved us from the powers of evil and came back when he was needed, so what I'm also saying is that you never really know the moments you are actually needed and when you are, you can accomplish great things."

"Thank you for your wisdom, uncle. I'll keep that in mind."

Rinaldo spares with Nevar for a time with breaks in between until the sun begins to set. At this time, Nevar makes the two dinner as they enjoy the sky and each other's company.

"I'm glad you're becoming a fine cook as well as a knight," Rinaldo says.

"Thank you for all you've taught me. I don't know what I would do without you," Nevar says with a gentle smile on his face.

"It's the least I can do. I just pray that I can stay the man you look up to and better. Ha! After all this talk about wanting to be more than what you are, you have me talking the same way. Another thing you should learn is that God provides us with the skills and resources necessary for the day's work. Don't worry about tomorrow because the same loving God that gave you the gifts of today will do the same for you tomorrow."

"I'll be sure to remember that as well and the many blessings I've already been given."

Nevar and Rinaldo go back to the barracks to rest for the day. Because of today's hard training, Nevar doesn't bother taking off his armor nor putting away his family's whip and just falls on his bed to immediately fall asleep. As he dreams, Nevar hears someone calling out to him. He doesn't know who this voice belongs to, but in his drowsiness, he follows it since it sounds familiar to him. Following it outside of the barracks to its source, Nevar looks around until he is directed by the voice to his horse. Again, he looks around for the source of the voice and begins to finally wake up.

"Wait, what am I doing here?" he asks himself.

It is then that he sees two hooded figures wandering around the area.

He asks them, "Hey, are you the night guards? Have you seen anyone around here or am I going crazy?"

"That's the son of Raven," one of the strangers whispers to the other.

"We should kill him and bring his head back as a reward," the other stranger whispers back.

"No, we should bring him back in pieces or force him to be like us like how we did with his father. Maybe make him into a serf. Perhaps, he will be different."

"Perhaps, we should have our fun with him first then go from there. Do you agree?"

"I agree. That is the better option."

The whispering of the two is barely audible to Nevar, so he takes out his whip and shakily prepares for a fight.

"Get out of here you two! You don't want to mess with someone like me," Nevar says in a failed attempt to intimidate them.

"What can you do to us, boy?"

"You're nothing like your father. You can't possibly do anything to us."

The two strangers reveal themselves to be vampires with hollow black eyes and skin as pale as the moon. This scares Nevar into taking action and whipping off the arm of one of them as the vampire narrowly manages to escape a quick death.

"You'll pay for that," the vampire says before charging at Nevar.

Thanks to his training, Nevar anticipates this and whips the vampire in half before it can reach him despite its inhuman speed. Following up his attack, Nevar whips the head off the second vampire before it can react to what happened to the first. Despite this display of skill that would impress anyone, Nevar stands frozen in fear unsure of what to do next because he fears if there are any more vampires lurking in the darkness. It is from this darkness that shadows leap out, but don't attack Nevar. Instead, after what feels like agonizing minutes of waiting, Nevar retreats back to the barracks to report the vampire attack, however, explosions and the sounds of fighting stop him from doing so.

All this sudden commotion scares Nevar's horse and by the time he takes his horse out of the stable, it runs off while not listening to his instructions and hardly goes where he wants it to as it tries to avoid the fighting. Nevar tries to make the most of this predicament by killing whatever vampires and beastmen that he comes across while appearing to look like a child on a horse. Eventually, his horse makes it outside of Rome where the vampires are attacking from. They come out of portals that connect to the place they're coming from.

"That's the son of Raven! Get him!" one vampire says.

"Why here of all places?" Nevar says as he still struggles to control his horse.

Because of all the vampires and beastmen around him, Nevar focuses on defending himself. Even while doing this, he can see an invisible force kill the enemies he can't reach and just assumes that a group of Rome's defenders are fighting alongside him. His horse charges through the enemy until it goes through the portal. This is where the horse finally listens to Nevar's instructions, but it is too late for him to go back through the portal as it has closed. Wondering exactly where he is so that he can get back home, Nevar looks around to see that he's in front of what's known as the Tower of Blasphemy.

"Of all the places to end up. Why, God, does it have to be here?" Nevar says as he begins to fear for his life.

This tower is home to most if not all vampires in the world where the most powerful vampire lords meet to coordinate their plans and make deals with one another. Its construction is otherworldly as different bits of large castles are grafted to it, and yet, it manages to stand with all its pieces set in place. At this moment of desperation for a way out, an angel manifests in front of Nevar. Two swords float by its side along with two eyes that each look into three directions at once. The angel's golden wings also float to its side with three bits of it floating downward like hanging crystals. It doesn't seem to have a face nor a body in its gold and black cloak. Instead, only a mouth and hands folded in prayer can be seen.

"Oh, thanks be to God you're here! Please, holy angel, you must get me out of here," Nevar says to it.

The angel's head twists in confusion in a way that a normal human head would break before it says. "Why would I do that? It is I who brought you here because God needs you to be here."

"Wait, was it your voice that I heard calling me in the night?"

"Yes, and I was the one leading your horse and defending you from the slaves of evil. I am your guardian angel."

"My guardian angel? It's an honor to finally see you after talking to you so much, but can you tell me why God wants me here?"

"Because you are to defeat the vampires and save the world from their influence like your father did."

"Me? I'm hardly one of the best knights. Even if I was, I'm only one man and that castle contains armies. It'd be better if I went back to Rome, helped them, and got their aid. We could also use the help of my uncle!"

"Do not worry about them nor your uncle. They will take care of themselves. You, on the other hand, have a task and an enemy before you."

"How can I possibly do this by myself?"

"You are not alone. I am here with you, your family and the saints in Heaven are interceding for you, the holy souls that you offered your rosary for are praying for you. God got you here and He will get you out. Are you beginning to lose your faith in Him?"

"No, not at all."

"Then you must proceed with the task at hand. Your destiny awaits you."

Nevar swallows his fear before looking at the tower that seems to reach past the clouds. He takes out his whip, grips it, then swings it down as if throwing away his cowardice and walks to the building hoping that God hasn't abandoned him to a terrible fate.

Chapter 2 – A Place of Self-Made gods

Inside the Tower of Blasphemy, Nevar cautiously

walks around as if the ground is covered in bits of glass

with very few safe places to step. The castle that he's

entered is currently full of beastmen, half human beasts,

and fully human serfs all of which are cleaning and

awaiting their orders. They watch Nevar with curiosity as

he doesn't seem to be their savior and is instead a fool who

wandered into the wrong place. Nevertheless, a birdman

serf informs his vampire lord of Nevar's arrival, which

makes the lord drop everything to meet the young man. The

lord is carried by his servants right to Nevar who jumps at the sight of him and takes the head off one of the serfs in response leading to the vampire lord falling on his face.

Trying to correct his mistake, Nevar tries to whip the vampire on the ground but misses again. The lord then hastily gets some distance between him and Nevar by retreating back and throwing his serfs at him that Nevar dispatches, however, he can't close the distance so he can kill the lord who is already at the top of a balcony.

"How rude. A host is supposed to introduce himself and make his guest feel comfortable as soon as they arrive," the vampire lord says.

"I don't need your introduction," Nevar says before really looking at the man's clothes. The vampire lord wears black and red robes with various twisted crosses decorating him similar to that of a royal bishop. "What bishop did you steal those clothes from?"

"I didn't steal these clothes. I was a royal bishop before I turned into a vampire. You don't seem to be the type of person who can be convinced with words to join my side, so I'll save you the speech and force you to become one of my servants instead."

More of the lord's serfs throw themselves at Nevar at their lord's command.

"Guardian angel, I'm going to need your help here," Nevar says.

"Jump," his angel says.

"Uh, okay? Woah!"

As soon as he jumps, he is thrown into the air and catches one of the many chandeliers in the room. Nevar jumps in between the chandeliers while being pushed in the right direction by his angel so that he doesn't fall. Meanwhile, the serfs jump from the higher floors to catch him while the flying ones are brought down by his angel and Nevar who can barely whip the serfs in mid-air and on the chandeliers. Eventually, Nevar gets close enough to the

vampire lord to whip his arm off so that he can't escape

through the door before he finishes him off by whipping

him in half, which was actually an attempt to whip off the

other arm that the lord was trying to use to open the door.

Nevar then attempts to jump to the balcony, but

only manages to get his foot on the railing before falling

off. His angel slows down his fall to the ground as the serfs

make a mad dash to leave the castle.

"That was easier than I thought it to be. It's all

thanks to God and to you," Nevar says to his angel.

"That was one of the first of many lords and the

lowest of them all. There's an apeman serf nearby still in

this castle that isn't leaving. He that will help you

understand it better and through some of your challenges.

Find him," his angel says.

Doing as his angel says, Nevar searches the castle

until he hears the noise of someone dropping and hitting

things. He cautiously follows the noise to its source until he finds an apeman trying out an armory of weapons. This apeman wears the attire of a priest with half of his body being that of a monkey.

"Hey! My guardian angel told me to find you," Nevar says to him.

The apeman looks at him strangely then says, "Really? I guess I can assume that's right from your earlier display, but still, I have my doubts. What do you want to know?"

"Can you tell me more about the tower?"

"What is there to say other than to be careful when you enter each castle? Every lord has their tricks in the event of an intruder entering. They even have rooms full of blessed weapons like these in the event that they want to betray a lord who shows weakness so they can take their possessions and serfs."

"That must've been why those serfs ran out the door. Why didn't you run?"

"Because I want the lords to pay for what they did to me. I was a respectable priest before I was kidnapped and forced to help them bless these weapons, be their serf, baptize the infants so they could kill them for their baptisms, and hear them pridefully embrace their sins as part of their blasphemous version of confession."

The apeman tries not to sob as he shakes in both anger and despair.

"I'm sorry you went through that."

"Don't be. I deserved it for being so weak as to allow them to force me to do it. Many times I could've said no. Many more times I could've chosen death over evil, but I didn't. Now, I will make things right."

"We can do this together."

"No, this is a penance I must do on my own. God has abandoned me to my weakness and will only take me back if I do this."

"He hasn't abandoned you. I'm-"

"Don't follow me, boy. Your guardian angel is enough company to protect you. I'll just slow you down."

The apeman runs out of the room at inhuman speeds similar to that of a vampire along with many blessed daggers.

"Wait!" Nevar says.

He chases the apeman going up staircase after staircase until he tires himself out.

"Do not worry about him. He'll soon repent and see the error of his ways," his guardian angel says.

"Yeah, but still, I want to help him."

Suddenly, serfs from the upper floors come down weapons already drawn.

"Get the son of Raven for our master!" one of the serfs says.

"Why am I always running into groups of people who want me?" Nevar asks himself before running back down the stairs while killing whatever serf that gets in his way. "I could use your help, my guardian angel!"

"You are on the right path. You do not need my help," his angel responds.

"If you say, so."

Nevar keeps running and tries to slow down the mob behind him by whipping the chandeliers above him in the hallways so they fall on them by the time they pass under them. This works, however, the mob doesn't start coming as more and more come to chase after him. Eventually, he comes to a dead end where there's only a door to a single room where trash, the dead bodies of serfs, and other vampires are in it along with a hatch to throw them in. Nevar enters the room then hastily barricades the door with the trash in the room and starts to panic to find his next move.

"What do I do now, angel? I could play dead among the bodies and hide myself in them, but that's too obvious," he says.

"Go down the hatch that the trash is dumped into," his angel answers.

Looking into the hatch, Nevar considers it then says, "I thought I was supposed to go up the tower, but-" At this time, the door is nearly open. "Okay, okay!"

Once he closes his nose, Nevar goes down the hatch and finds himself where he expected, a place full of rotting corpses and trash. He gets up and wades through the corpses until he hears the sound of something moving in the pile. Mutilated corpses from the pile that are somehow still alive then emerge ready to drag Nevar in with them. Nevar fights them off until he can get to solid ground and exit the room. The hallways and rooms of this castle are

Venatores Noctis: Chronicles of a Royal Hunting Family

predictably less luxurious than the previous one above it

since it appears to be more like a combination of a hospital,

garbage disposal site, and an alchemist's lab than a place

for a royal lord.

Further in, Nevar finds many mutilated beastmen,

people, and even vampires twisted and turned into furniture

and used as decorations. A single one of these serfs breaks

his bones until he is back to normal and introduces himself

to Nevar.

"I am the lord of this castle. I must thank you for

ridding the tower of that pompous ex-bishop so that I may

take his place. As thanks, I will let you leave this section of

the castle without being harmed. I will even tell you that

some of my underlings will not listen to me, so you should

be careful around them, which I'm sure you may already be

aware of," the half beast half vampire man says.

Part of the beastman was ape-like and another part

was like that of a lion. His head is that of a wolf while his legs are that of a goat. This entire mismatch of body parts leaves Nevar speechless as he tries to comprehend this lord's appearance, whether or not he is speaking the truth, and how he can possibly be a lord.

"I thought serfs couldn't become lords," Nevar says.

"Through hard work and some well intentioned backstabbing, I became a lord. A lord of the lowest castle, but still a lord nevertheless."

"Still, I thought lords can only be vampires."

"They can. The thing is that I improved my body before I became a vampire. It's one of the favors that I did for the lords before I became one and it's one that I gladly accepted. You see, serfs are constantly experimented on so that the vampire lords can have strong defenders and fodder to throw at their enemies, but vampires cannot improve their original bodies once they take their blasphemous baptism. Their bodies can only be cut by blessed weapons and this makes them unable to be experimented on and turned into a half beastman half vampire such as I."

"I see. Nevertheless, I must shun your thanks because I am bound by divine command to destroy the vampire lords in this tower."

"You said that you see, but do you really? Look at me and look around you. The vampire serfs that I have are no mere weaklings. They were once great vampire lords that had their own castles that were above mine. Look at yourself. I can see the fear inside you as you struggle even to stand still."

"That doesn't matter. I still have to do this."

"Suit yourself then. I can always use another serf, a piece of art, or furniture in my castle. You'll make a fine first trophy of mine on my ascent to the top."

If Nevar were to be honest with himself, he doesn't know what he was talking about and was going to take the lord's offer, and yet, his duty compels him to fight. The vampire lord moves faster to Nevar's surprise as Nevar misses the first strike leading to Nevar being punched in the stomach and sent falling backward while still standing.

"Ah, I thought that would've knocked you down," the lord compliments.

"I have a good teacher that taught me to stay standing," Nevar says.

"You won't be standing for long."

Nevar tries attacking faster to catch the vampire lord and manages to just scratch him because of his speed. He keeps up the attack so that the lord cannot get in another attack, however, he doesn't see a way that he can hit him. In a moment of inspired risky creativity, Nevar hits the chandelier of skulls where he thinks the lord is going to land based on his pattern of dodging. His guess is correct as the lord is unable to change his direction mid-air leading to him falling to the ground and Nevar being able to get a hit in. This isn't enough to kill the lord as he is still able to

Venatores Noctis: Chronicles of a Royal Hunting Family

stand despite being nearly cut in half. The lord lacks an arm, half their body, and face, but still has both legs.

"That was good, boy. Tell me your name so that I can distinguish you between my top serfs," the lord says. To answer him, Nevar attempts to finish the man off but misses as the lord anticipated his attack and dodges out of the way at such a fast speed that makes it look like his severe injuries don't matter. "I shall call you Stubborn or Stupid. Stub-id maybe. I'll give the name some more thought once I've torn you apart and put you back together in an appropriate way."

The lord then leaps at Nevar until he is caught midair by the apeman priest who stabs his blessed daggers into the lord's head and heart. Once on the ground, the priest stabs more daggers into the lord's chest to finally kill him.

"Did you need to stab him that many times?" Nevar asks.

"Yes, he had multiple hearts," the priest responds, "I'm sorry it took so long for me to get here. There were many serfs to sneak around."

"Thank you for your help! I never got your name. My name is Nevar."

"Nevar…Nevar. Oh, do you happen to be the son of Saint Raven the hero?"

"I am!"

"Your father's fighting style inspired my own. I used to be a warrior priest in the prime of my life. My inspirations are people like your father and his friend, Confessor Rinaldo. I'm sure you're familiar with him as well?"

"Yes, my uncle taught me how to fight."

"No wonder why you were able to hold your own then. Anyways, you shouldn't be down here. Instead, you should get to the heart of the tower that lies in the center of it above and destroy it so that the entire tower will crumble."

"But that won't kill all the vampire lords."

"Sure, but it'll get them out here and force them to fight amongst themselves. They can hardly live with each other now with so many possessions. Imagine how they would live with none."

"So, why did you come down here?"

"To save you and to kill this particular lord. He's the one that experiments on most of the serfs. With him dead, a good majority of serfs will be free from his torture and the lords above will lack his powerful creations. Also, you're heading in the wrong direction. Beneath and to the side of us are more castles known as the underworld castles for the lower lords."

"Ah, I see. Thank you!"

"Don't mention it and don't get into trouble again."

"Wait, before you go, you have to tell me your name."

"No, I don't. It's not worth remembering. Continue to ascend the tower while I grow a rebellion of serfs. I pray that you succeed, Nevar Aurora, son of Saint Raven."

The apeman priest leaps away from Nevar.

"I guess he's right. Having more people to fight would help," Nevar says to himself.

"He is. Though your paths are separate, they will still cross and you'll aid each other when the time comes. Speaking of that, you are going to meet another who will aid you soon. Someone who will help you for the rest of your life and will be your wife," his angel says.

"Really?! I must meet her then."

"Hurry. She is in the next castle above us and needs your help. I will guide you to her."

"I will!"

Venatores Noctis: Chronicles of a Royal Hunting Family

With a new exciting goal, Nevar rushes ahead without question in the hopes that he'll finally have help in this destiny of his gleefully ignorant of the future horrors and challenges that lie in wait for him as news of his arrival and defeat of two vampire lords conspire against him and against themselves for the glory of killing the son of Raven Aurora.

Chapter 3 – Saving a Soul on the Edge

Many serfs come after Nevar, and yet, he barrels through them all as the fear that was in him is completely buried at the prospect of finding his wife to be and a helper in his destiny. He doesn't even notice the hanging bodies some of which are still alive used as decorations in the castle that his angel says his wife is in. Because of this, it's a complete surprise to him to find his wife to be skinned alive and hanging from the ceiling with hooks in her hands and feet.

Stunned by this, Nevar says, "Is…is she even alive?"

The fear of his situation begins to enter him again as he finally realizes what's around him. Bodies and the skins of humans, vampires, and serfs alike decorate this castle. This morbid sight is contrasted by the beautiful furniture, statues, and paintings that would typically decorate the house of a royal who would buy exotic and expensive items from across the world. All of this is being cleaned by the serfs in an attempt to keep all the normal furniture clean and the morbid ones somewhat clean.

"Yes, she is alive, but just barely. She is kept alive by dark sciences and her own will to survive strengthened by her God-given power as she was told that her husband to be would save her. You must find the girl that is wearing her skin, take it back, and give it back to your wife to be," Nevar's guardian angel says.

"Okay! Please, point me in her direction!"

Nevar's guardian angel turns into a light that shines ahead of him to guide him in the right direction. To his surprise, the serfs in the castle don't go after him and are instead going to other places to fulfill their duty with some even fighting each other for a reason he'll find out soon. The hallways and rooms he is guided through subtly change and sometimes massively change with some being completely morbid with bodies both dead and alive in them and others having mostly furniture and art. He doesn't think too long about why this is especially since he almost runs into a vampire lord that leaps by him. It seems like he's going to have to fight them until he sees the blessed weapon in the lord's hand and wonders why they would have it. The lord then leaps past him and clashes weapons with another lord.

"You'll never inherit grandfather's inheritance!" one says to the other.

"And you've held on to mother's possessions for far too long! I will be the favored son of the family then its ruler!" the other responds.

Seeing this display of infighting makes Nevar unsure of what to do.

One of the lords looks at him then says, "Get involved in this and you die!"

Unsure of what to do, Nevar looks up to where his guardian angel's light is and sees that it's away from the fighting.

"I'm sorry! I'll leave you two alone then!" Nevar says with his hands up.

He then follows his guardian angel's light through fights of vampire lords fighting each other. Some of these lords are clearly wearing human skin like hunters in the wild wearing the skin of their prey. This sight makes Nevar anxious hoping that his guardian angel's light shines over one of them so that he can save his wife to be. Eventually, he does find the lord that his guardian angel's light shines over. This lord is a young woman about the same age as him who wears a purple dress decorated in warped crosses, gold stars, and stained with blood along with the skin that he was looking for. She's in a room not decorated in the slighted with corpses as decorates but with corpses on the floor of a recent fight that she is still finishing with another lord. The young woman is not at all concerned with Nevar's arrival, but the other lord is distracted and gets his arm cut off. She then tries to finish him off as the two lock blades with the other lord desperately trying to hold her off with its one last arm that holds its blade with sweaty hands.

"There…there he is," the injured lord says, "The son of Raven Aurora. He's the one we should be killing-"

"Shut up! I decide who I want to kill and it's going to be you! Your allies and you interrupted our family's fight for each other's possessions and for that, you will die!" the young lord responds before killing the other.

After cutting off the lord's head, the young woman spits on the vampire's corpse before cleaning his blood off her blade.

She then begins to walk by Nevar while saying, "I don't care who you are. Get out of my way and I'll let you leave this tower just to spite the other lords."

"I...I won't let you leave! You have the skin of my wife to be so you must give it back," Nevar says as he prepares for a fight.

The young woman stops walking and appears to be visibly furious as her skin suit stretches because of it.

"That girl...that wretch is your wife to be? She is nothing more than an overrated peasant! Your 'wife to be' was loved unjustly by everyone in the town we lived in and enjoyed every second of it. The only thing she's worthy of is a slow death!"

"Even if you're telling the truth, she's my wife to be. I'll love her no matter what."

"Then you'll die a slow death like her."

Blinded by her emotions, the lord charges at Nevar without considering his skill and loses a leg because of it and is then quickly finished off by him whipping her head off.

"She must've been incredibly angry if she was this reckless. How am I going to take the skin off her?" Nevar says.

"The young woman had gone through many battles today as you can see and her fury at your wife to be led her to disregard her safety," Nevar's angel says.

"Can you help me take my wife to be's skin off her? I don't know how to do it myself."

"That is no problem for me. I'll reattach it to your wife to be as well."

"Thank you so much. It would've been too much and too meticulous of a process for me to handle."

"Come, let us hurry to her."

"Right!"

Hurrying back to his wife to be, Nevar follows his guardian angel while also defending himself from relatives of the young woman he defeated who swear their vengeance on him. Thanks to the help of his guardian angel, he is able to defeat every lord and serf in his way flowing through them as if they were no more than a stationary obstacle than a living one, and make it back to his wife to be in time. His angel's light envelops his wife to be as it reattaches her skin to her while taking her off the hooks in her hands and feet. Finally, Nevar's wife to be has her skin on her body with stitches keeping it together. Nevar covers her nakedness with a nearby purple curtain and helps her sit up as she awakes.

"Hey, are you okay?" Nevar asks her.

Being this close to her lets Nevar see that she doesn't exactly have the kind of appearance that would turn heads even if her skin wasn't stitched on her body, however, something radiating from her that Nevar can't see makes her a wonder to behold. The young girl opens her eyes and is surprised to be alive and safe with her skin on her body as she looks at it as if she's seeing it for the very first time.

She then looks at Nevar and asks, "Who are you? Are you my husband to be that God promised me?"

"I am. My name is Nevar. What's yours?"

"Vanina. Ah, do you know what happened to the girl that took my skin?"

"You won't have to worry about her anymore. I killed her."

"You did?"

"What's the matter? You sound sad."

"I did feel sad for her despite what she did for me. Is that strange to say?"

"Yes, it is. Why would you feel sad for a vampire like her?"

"When we were younger, she was always jealous of me for whatever reason. Maybe it's because people would always come to me to help them? I was popular in my hometown because I'd help anyone who'd ask and didn't ask. It couldn't have been because she was jealous of the way I look. I'm not that pretty after all especially now."

"That's nonsense. I think you're pretty despite your scars."

"People always said that the radiance of my soul showed on my body, which I thought was a funny compliment. Still, the girl must've worn my skin thinking that she captured what other people saw. One day while we were in here, she came to me to complain that my skin wasn't working for her even though she said that she made her family proud by doing what she did. She still couldn't become the center of attention like she wanted."

"That's what happens when you just see things on the surface. Now, come on. I have to bring you to safety."

"There he is! There's the one that murdered one of our own and brought the other lords upon us during our sacred fight!" a vampire lord says as many of them enter the roof with their serfs.

Even though they are surrounded, Nevar still stands up ready to fight, and yet, he finds that his fear begins to overtake him as he feels that he is unable to move. He keeps telling himself to move, but his body won't listen to him. Now, of all times, he is unsure what to do and most afraid because he doesn't know how to protect himself in a way that would save both himself and Vanina. At the very least, they would end up wounded, which would make the rest of their journey next to impossible to complete as if it doesn't appear that way already.

"Blessed Mother, come to our aid!" Vanina calls out.

A small light that the lords are blind to starts to shine within Vanina as she prays.

"The deluded girl will think her lady will save her when her praying hasn't worked before!" a vampire lord mockingly says.

The lords then leap on the two, however, a barrier of light sharp as swords form around them and pierce the lords and their serfs while leaving Nevar and Vanina unharmed. With the threats to the two now dead, the swords of light disappear.

"That was amazing!" Vanina says as she jumps to her feet and is additionally surprised by this. "I can stand too! It feels like nothing happened to me!"

"Glory be to God," Nevar says in a somewhat less than enthusiastic tone.

"What's wrong?"

"Nothing, nothing at all actually. I'm really happy that you're feeling okay and your prayers were answered. It's just that…I'm disappointed that I froze up and didn't act as fast as I should've. It's stupid to be concerned about that and I'll do better I know. Forget I said anything."

"No, I get it. I was losing my faith off and on when I was hanging without my skin and without any sign of hope."

"But I'm expected to be better. I'm expected to be brave."

"I think you're the bravest man I know for coming here to save me."

"Thank you. That really helps me. Now, we should get you out of here."

"Why? I can help."

"That barrier only happened once. How do we know it will manifest again?"

"It will when God wills it," Nevar's guardian angel interrupts, "She will go with you and be integral to your victory."

The angel then disappears as fast as it appeared.

"You see? I should go with you."

"Okay, okay. I'll allow it because my guardian angel says so."

"That was your guardian angel?"

"Yes, it got me here and has been helping me through this entire thing. It even put your skin back on."

"Wow. Thank you, angel!"

"You're welcome," the angel says as it appears then disappears again, which gets a chuckle out of Vanina and Nevar.

The two exit the room and continue their way upward through the castle. Along the way, they find that the lords and their serfs are still fighting each other despite recent events.

"Why do they keep fighting each other?" Nevar says.

"Vampire lords are vain, in general, especially this family. They want whatever their sinful hearts crave and this family wanted fame, fortune, possessions, and more. It's one of the reasons why I felt bad for the girl that skinned me alive. She was pressured by her family to go above and beyond and nothing she did could truly satisfy them."

"I'm still surprised you feel bad for her."

"I'm surprised as well. A priest that I visited once said that it's a particular God-given grace that makes me feel the same way that Christ did for us when He was crucified that being feeling pity for those who don't deserve it."

"That is a great blessing. It's no wonder why your soul radiates so much."

"It's all thanks to my family, my parish, and my devotion to Our Lady, her husband, the saints I pray to, and the holy souls in Purgatory."

As the two continue on their way up, some of the lords and serfs decide to go after them, however, they are undefeatable together. Nevar's strength and skills are boosted by having Vanina around him and her compliments of his fighting abilities. That is not to say that she doesn't help as her blessing activates when she pray to the Blessed Mother and when that doesn't work, she uses the blessed weapons on the ground and gets in the fight when she can. When she can't, she breaks the expensive statues, vases, and other novelties in the castle to distract the lords of this castle so that Nevar can easily kill them. Eventually, the two come across the apeman priest and his freed serfs.

"Father, wait up!" Nevar says to the priest.

"It's good to see you're okay in this vampire lord civil war madness. Who is this with you?"

"I am his wife to be, Vanina," Vanina says.

"Did the vampires take your wedding rings? I could send some of my serfs to help you find them."

"Oh, no. We just met," Nevar says, "My guardian angel brought us together and helped me save her life, and the Blessed Mother even saved us."

"I shouldn't even be surprised that miraculous things happen around you, Nevar. I think I've gathered enough serfs to attack the center of it to bring this tower to the ground."

"We'll join you in your assault."

"I expect it, but we have our own way of doing it that I've already put in effect, so you should take your own way. You already have enough help in Heaven, whereas we slaves need to make it up for ourselves first."

The apeman priest runs away to join the serfs that he's leading.

"Wait, hold on! You still haven't told me your name!"

"He must be confident about our victory."

"He's also stubborn about not working together. We should get going as fast as we can since they're already attacking the center."

Nevar and Vanina hurry on their way to their destiny while the vampire lords now realize the threat approaching them and decide to make plans for it.

Fan art of Nevar by @ArtistsSouthern (on Twitter)

Chapter 4 – Deaths and Lives of Our Own Making

As Nevar and Vanina continue upward, they come

across dead serfs with their bodies completely destroyed as

if they were killed by a sadist.

"What happened here?" Nevar says.

He continues forward before he is pushed back by

his angel. A trap is activated as spikes come from the rug

underneath him before the trap automatically hides itself.

"You have to be more careful!" Vanina says while clinging on to one of Nevar's arms.

"Okay, okay I will!"

Despite Nevar's heart feeling like it's going to burst out of his chest he feels out where he should go. There are many places on the ground that activate the traps, but there are certain ones spread apart that just appear to be solid ground.

"I'll go first again," Nevar says.

Nevar then nervously steps on one of the supposedly safe places on the floor only for it to activate a fire trap on the wall that he manages to duck under just in time.

"What are we supposed to do if every part of the ground activates a trap?" Nevar says.

Vanina thinks about a possible solution while feeling the floor and looking around for possible clues. Nothing in particular separates this castle from the others besides the color of the wallpaper, the paintings, and various other decorations, but the paintings that depict ballroom dancers catch Vanina's attention.

"I think we have to move like the dancers," Vanina says.

"What makes you think that?" Nevar wonders.

"Just look at how the leg of one of the dancers lines up with the places in the floor that doesn't activate a trap and the ones ahead of it have the same dancers looking like they continue the dance."

Okay, but we're still going to have to guess where the next one is. Perhaps we should just find another castle to approach the center from. Maybe there's even a secret way around the trap."

"But the apeman and the other serfs are already attacking the center and we may not get there in time. Besides, your angel and my barriers could protect us if we make a mistake."

"I wouldn't test them to protect us if we're doing something that we shouldn't."

"I have a good feeling that we should. There has to be a better way."

"I see that there are claw marks on the walls and ceiling so the serfs could've been crawling on them, but they could have traps on them as well and we can't crawl on them like they can. What better option is there?"

"…alright. I guess there's nothing better. God, please protect us in this risky plan."

Nevar takes Vanina's hand and the two begin to move in the same way as the paintings of the dancers depict. They move in the direction that the dancers seem to be moving in while hesitating only for a few seconds to make sure the next part of the floor isn't a trap. This works surprisingly well as the two begin to smile and actually enjoy dancing with one another. Even though they have to guess at certain points because of the blood on the paintings, they manage to get far until the point where this is no other painting.

Seeing this ahead of them, Nevar points this out then says, "What do we do?"

"Uh. Umm. Take a guess?" Vanina answers.

"Tch. Why couldn't these vampires complete this collection of paintings of all things?"

When the two get to the place where there is no painting, Nevar hesitates to move as he feels out the floor whereas Vanina wants to just guess.

"Hold on, we still have a second-"

"The second is up!"

Vanina moves them forward while silently praying. A barrier then forms around them as dozens of spikes hit it. The spikes then recede and their barrier dissipates once they are safe.

"That was too close," Nevar says while continuously shaking and trying to shake off his fear.

"You think? I'm just glad to be alive," Vanina says.

After shaking off what just happened, the two go through a door. For the rest of the way up, there are no traps. There aren't even lords or serfs that get in their way as most are already dead. Going further up shows the two the answer as to why. Opportunistic vampire lords and serfs, and normal serfs rebel against their masters either for power, to escape, or to join the rebellion against the lords of the tower. Taking advantage of this, Nevar and Vanina head closer to the center to find that the previous masters of the tower have been overthrown by more powerful lords. The apeman priest and his serfs fight against these lords.

In an attempt to help, Nevar and Vanina join the fight. Numbers are the serf's greatest weapon as the lords squash and kill them as if they were swatting flies. Some of the serfs attempt to go for the living heart in the center of the room that's keeping the tower together, however, the lords are too quick and kill these serfs. Seeing that the heart is more than a decoration and the primary target, Nevar shoots his shot at attacking it and manages to hit it several times. Unbeknownst to him and some of the others, castles start falling off the tower because of this and bury themselves in the ground, and crash into the castles below the ground. A vampire lord notices what Nevar is doing and goes after him for an instant kill but is intercepted by the apeman priest who takes the lethal blow for him.

"Why?" Nevar says without really knowing what to say.

The priest's guardian angel then manifests and decimates the vampire lord that struck him into bits.

"I can't let a soul as brilliant as yours die so soon when you have so much to do. As for me, I guess God favored me more than I thought. My doubts were my worst sin, but it looks like I don't need to worry about that anymore. I'll see you later, son of Raven. Oh, and my name is Josiah since you wanted to know so badly."

Life then leaves the priest's body as his guardian angel goes to him and carries his soul upward until both disappear.

"Nevar!" Vanina says as she runs to his aid.

Her barrier of swords protects them since the rest of the serfs are dead. Five lords are left who fiercely attack them both in an attempt to protect the tower and gain the glory of being the one to kill them.

"Thank you, Vanina! I'll finish this!"

Thanks to Vanina's help, Nevar can continuously damage the heart of the tower. Even as a lord slips through the barrier, Nevar does not let this scare him and uses his finishing blow to whip both the lord and the heart in half. With the heart destroyed, the lords of the tower begin to take whatever valuables they have if they haven't already begun to get up and leave. In this chaos, Nevar and Vanina run as fast as they can as the castles crumble into the ground. Vanina's barrier protects them from the debris as they continue in whatever direction seems correct. What they may know is that the castle they're in is falling to the ground as the others in the air are. As the castle falls, the room around them rotates, but they still manage not to be thrown around. They go from castle to destroyed castle in their desperate and blind attempt to survive.

Eventually, the castle they're in falls onto the ground. The cushions of the overly expensive couches break their fall along with Vanina's barrier. They continue upward as they use the rubble as makeshift stairs until they break out of the castle and on to solid ground just as the rest of the castle sinks into the ground.

"Talk about a fall from grace. I thought we would never stop falling," Nevar says.

"At least we're finally safe," Vanina says.

"Yeah, why don't you turn off your barrier then?"

"The Blessed Mother and God have more control over it than I do so there must be a reason-"

A vampire lord leaps out from the dirt and punches Vanina a fair distance away. Thankfully, she isn't too hurt because of her barrier's protection, but now she is too far away from Nevar to help him. Nevar tries to hit the lord with his whip as the vampire dodges his strikes until he's able to get some distance between him.

"Oh my. You are your father's son. It's not too late to make up for what you did. Become a vampire, help me dig up the remains of the tower, and we will rule the world as we once did," the lord says.

"Who even are you?" Nevar asks.

"Someone who will be the master of this world."

"I didn't even see you defending the heart of the tower. How important can you really be?"

"More important than you think, boy. While those fools were defending a tower that was already killing itself, I was attending to my own strength. Behold the fruits of my labor."

The area around the vampire lord's hands darkens like a cloud forming in the sky before he raises them to the sky to darken it. Nevar's and Vanina's heads begin to hear the temptations of demons as they feel their strength begin to leave them.

"So, what's it going to be?" the lord asks.

"I'll never accept your offer," Nevar says while attempting to attack the lord.

Now that his strength is lessened, Nevar is even slower at trying to attack the lord and misses more than usual. It doesn't help that this entire ordeal has pushed him to its limits either.

"Give up. I can tell you're afraid of me."

"That's right. I am afraid of you. I was afraid of nearly everything in that tower, and yet, I kept fighting because I was more afraid of sinning against God and letting the people who love me down."

"So, it's fear that drives you. How pathetic."

"No, it's not fear that drives me. It's my love of God, family, and friends that push me forward when I would rather just cower in fear and do nothing."

"That's even worse. You know what? I don't think I need you anymore."

"Then try to take my life."

Nevar lets go of his fears while whipping the ground to signify him letting it go. The lord then charges at him until his arms suddenly come off because of Nevar's guardian angel. This stops the lord right in front of Nevar who he is now visibly afraid of.

He then leaps back and says, "You think this is over?! It isn't. I mutated my body before I became a lord. Any second now, I will-"

Multiple arms replace the arms that the lord lost. The mutations don't stop there as the lord loses both legs and gains four arms in their place. In addition, he gains two more arms that sprout out of his shoulder and one more that comes out of his mouth. He then charges at Nevar confident of his victory. Meanwhile, Nevar is calm and confident as his senses are boosted beyond that of a vampire by his faith in God. Because of this, he perceives everything in slow motion up until the point where he strikes the vampire. After the first strike, the lord is too afraid to move since his pride was shattered along with a majority of his body with that one strike. Nevar then unleashes a fury of whips to finish off the lord. The darkness disappears when the lord dies as the night sky gives way to the morning sun.

Vanina finally reaches Nevar and the two embrace and kiss one another. Horses approach them from a distance led by Rinaldo who almost falls on his face while dismounting his horse to embrace Nevar as well.

"Thanks be to God infinity times infinity that you're alive!" Rinaldo says with held back tears flowing from his eyes.

"I'm glad you're safe too, uncle," Nevar says.

"Did you destroy the entire tower by yourself?"

"No, I did it with the help of my wife to be, Vanina along with a saintly priest, named Josiah, my guardian angel, and the intercession of Heaven."

"Of course, of course! There was never a doubt in my mind that you would accomplish great things."

"Really? There were plenty of doubts in my mind."

The three of them laugh before heading back to Rome. Since the remainder of the tower and lower tower are still beneath the ground, the site of it becomes heavily guarded by the best soldiers of the Church just in case more vampires spring out from it, but what they don't know is that the vampires and their serfs are too busy weeding out the weak among them before they'll make their move on the surface. Nevar is celebrated as a hero and is married to Vanina shortly after. Josiah and the many serfs that helped Nevar are given graves at a graveyard where many saints are buried. Meanwhile, many vampires and their serfs still plague the lands during the night.

This makes Nevar dedicate his family to the eradication of them and all that is evil on the earth as he says to the excitement of a zealous crowd, "From this day forth, my family and I will hunt the night! May God's will be done on Earth as it is in Heaven."

The End

Concept art of Nevar Aurora.

𝕭𝖊𝖍𝖎𝖓𝖉 𝖙𝖍𝖊 𝕾𝖙𝖔𝖗𝖞

- Nevar's appearance is inspired by Trevor Belmont's appearance both in the *Castlevania* games and in the anime.

- The events of this story are somewhat inspired by *Castlevania 3*'s in how the main character meets different characters and is the starting point for the family's vampire hunting legacy.

- This story is also closest to the general stories of Castlevania games in how the main character travels in a castle infested by vampires and monsters.

- The line "hunt the night" is taken from *Castlevania: Lament of Innocence* where Leon says that his clan will hunt the night. It is also the inspiration for the title of this series, which means Hunters of the Night in English.

Venatores Noctis: Selfless Self-Destruction

"Life is Suffering. Rest is for the Dead."

Albert Oon

Chapter 1 – A Legacy to Live Up to

A lone man in a black cloak stops at a town on his way to his destination.

"Can you spare any food or water?" he asks in various ways to the townspeople he comes across.

Everyone who sees him is wary of the man since he doesn't show his face and because he has pale skin like that of a vampire. His cloak is stained with dirt and blood, and he stinks of sweat. It doesn't help that the vampires have recently taken their fair share of the infants, priests, and young for their blasphemous sacraments and to make more serfs. A nearby scream attracts the attention of the lone man who runs to find out what the reason behind it is. He finds a crowd gathered around a vampire that's holding a bloody infant.

"I've ripped this infant from his mother's womb because you would not pay your due tithe to us. Let this be your final lesson or else it will happen again and it will only get worse from there," the vampire says with the crying twitching infant held in the air like a trophy.

It is then the lone man takes off his cloak, jumps into the air, and slices the vampire in two at the torse with his whip before catching the infant, wrapping him in his cloak, and giving him to a relative. Now that his cloak is off, the townspeople can clearly see who this lone man is.

"It's Claudius Aurora of the Aurora vampire hunting family!" a townsperson says.

Most people in the crowd are glad to see him except for another band of vampire hunters that approach him.

"I didn't expect the son of a coward to be out here by himself," one of the hunters says.

"I'd hit you in the face, but I don't want to stain my hands with the blood of a vile sinner who would insult my father," Claudius responds in kind.

Claudius passes by the hunters.

"If your father was on the field rather than comfortable in the political sphere then we would actually respect him," another hunter says.

"Ignore him. Our job is done here," yet another says.

"Our job is done? He took our job."

"They'll be another. I say that we follow him and return the favor he did for us."

The words of the hunter are ignored as Claudius is on his way out of the town.

He is stopped by a townsperson that says, "We didn't know it was you asking for food and water, so here's some. We have more if this isn't enough."

"No, as it said, if you do not help the least, you do not help the Lord. This town deserved to be tormented by the vampires," Claudius coldly says while taking the food and water and throwing them on the ground.

The townsperson recoils in fear with the others who hear what Claudius has said. Meanwhile, Claudius' stomach growls. He offers up the pain of his hunger and thirst before continuing on. As he travels to his next destination, he asks a traveling merchant for food and water to which the merchant gives it even though Claudius can't pay for it. With a drooling mouth, Claudius almost devours the bread from the hands of the merchant, but he stops himself, thanks God for the bread and water, and then calmy eats and drinks.

"Haven't you eaten anything, boy?" the merchant asks.

"No, not since the last daily mass I attended," Claudius says.

"I mean food like meat, vegetables, and non-consecrated bread."

"I haven't since I left Rome."

"Rome? That's a week's journey from here. You've gone this long without food or water?"

"It's been a three day journey thanks to the kindness of strangers."

"How can you survive like that?"

"By the gifts of God and strangers. I've drunk from rivers and lakes and eaten the leftover pieces of bread from those who could offer it."

"Why are you putting yourself through this? I mean have you taken a look at yourself in a while? Are you some kind of warrior penitential monk?"

"No, I have just taken many penances on my quest so that I may pay for my sins, the sins of the world, and for the Holy Souls in Purgatory along the way. These scars that you see on me are self-inflicted such as my bruised and bloodied knees from intense praying and mediation. I tattooed and cut the cross and monogram of Our Lord on my chest both as penance and as a sign of who I've given my soul to. This hundred decade rosary on my right arm is here for me always pray to the Blessed Mother, and these bandage on my face is meant to conceal my identity so people won't treat me better because of my upbringing."

"Who are you exactly?"

"Claudius Aurora."

"Oh, Aurora. I've heard that your father and his band of vampire hunters have really helped the allies of the Church and more. Why aren't you back in Rome with him where it's much safer and more comfortable?"

"Because I must live up to my grandfather's legacy. It's right that I should be since I'm his grandson. He always said that I would do great things and become even better than he was when he was alive on Earth. I'm not going to let him down." Claudius falls to his knees and looks towards the sky. "Grandfather Nevar, look down upon me with favor, and please intercede for me in Heaven."

After parting ways, Claudius sees a party of vampires and their serfs making their way toward the town he was in. Because of how they treated him, he decides to ignore it. A ray of light shines on him as an angel appears in front of him, his guardian angel. This divine being manifests itself as a being with a cloak made of thorny vines, four wings and four whips that float independently of the body, and four eyes with no mouth that reside in the dark hood.

It says, "Be merciful, Claudius. There are repentant souls in the town now because of your actions. They are now worthy of having their punishment lifted from them for the time being."

"Is that so? A harsher punishment could further prevent them from being uncharitable to strangers," Claudius says.

"The vampires will not take kindly to one of their own being killed and the people that they spare will become their serfs. This town won't last a day."

"Becoming a serf is a horrible fate. Okay, you've convinced me. I'll go."

Meanwhile, the vampire hunting group from before eagerly awaits the approaching vampires and sets up a trap for them. The archers perch themselves on the roofs while the warriors and assassins lurk in the shadows or act as live bait. This trap works in taking out a vampire and some of the serfs, however, the vampires have brought their best since they heard that a member of the Aurora family is headed this way and the hunters are soon killed. Each of them is killed in brutal ways with some being beaten to death with their own limbs. A survivor is left alive and forced to crawl to the approaching Claudius with his arm being the only limb he has to pull him forward. The townspeople fearfully hide in their homes and pray that Claudius is successful.

"Please…help. I don't want to die," the dying hunter says.

Looking down at him, Claudius says, "Vampire hunting is a job, not a lucrative career choice because it will one day end forever. I hope you know that now. There's no saving your life, so use the shameful state you are in as penance and hopefully, God will save your soul. Perhaps you won't even go to Purgatory."

After leaving the hunter to their fate, Claudius boldly approaches the vampires and readies his whip for the fight. The vampires who are hungry for a glorious victory of taking the head of an Aurora leap into action and are swiftly killed by Claudius. He whips them in half then sighs at the lack of challenge. It is then that the other vampires use a pincer attack on him and try to attack him one after the other in an unpredictable pattern. Still, Claudius is able to dodge and kill each vampire thanks to his training. When the dust settles, the townspeople come out of hiding and cheer.

"You have seen the fruits of faith and will of God shown through me. Go and sin no more," Claudius says before heading off.

It is then that a townsperson offers him a horse and satchel of bread, which he reluctantly accepts because of the silent whispers of his guardian angel. He then crosses himself in thanks for the gifts and heads out while silently praying his rosary.

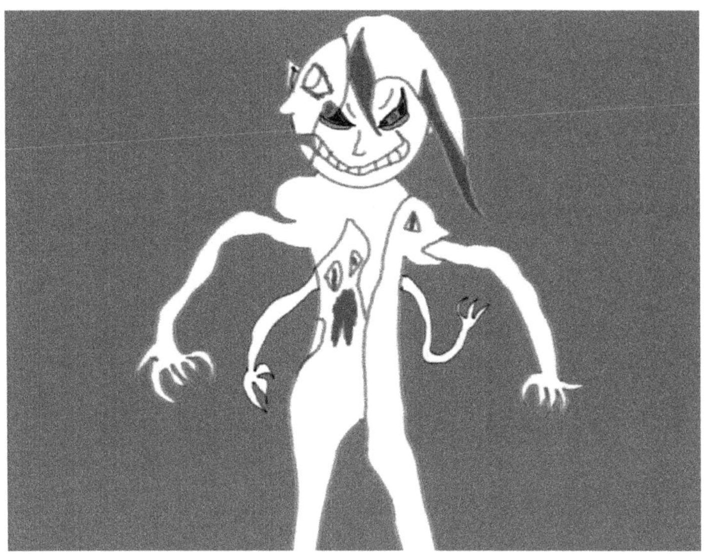

Chapter 2 – Pitiable Self-Made Kings

Along the way to his destination, Claudius feeds pieces of the bread that he has to the animals he comes across and then to a wandering blind priest who he eats the last of his bread with underneath a cloudy night sky.

"Thank you for the bread, young man. You are a gift from God," the priest says.

"It's the least I can do. Penitential priests like you inspired me to do the same as you," Claudius says.

"Are you a blind penitential like me?"

"No, but I do fast and practice self-flagellation like you. I took up these practices to purify my soul and do penance for many on my quest."

"What quest is this that can allow you to take on a similar penance to mine in addition to it?"

"The quest to live up to my grandfather, Nevar Aurora's, legacy by slaying the vampires in the upside down Tower of Blasphemy. He destroyed the tower on the surface, but the lower tower is still beneath the earth and has been monitored by the Church for decades. Now, I go to destroy the lower tower as my grandfather destroyed the upper, especially since Rome hasn't heard back from those that monitor the tower in some time and reports coming from this region tell us that the vampires' serfs are out kidnapping the poor."

"This quest is great and too large for you to embrace similar penances to mine. You should fill yourself with food and stop whipping yourself so that you're at full strength when you face the enemy."

"I fill myself with whatever God gives me and deny excesses."

"Are you sure you're not denying yourself gifts that God has given you to help you along the way?"

"I'm sure of it because I follow your example."

"My purpose is one that not many should follow just as your grandfather had his own purpose that only he could do. I'm assuming you prayed and meditated for a long time on your purpose like I do?"

"Of course."

"Then I hope to God that you're following God's will rather than your own."

"If I was following my own will, then things would've been easier."

"Just know that not everything that's harder to do is essentially holy and be open to correction. Keep your pride in check and remember that we all still sin and make mistakes. Even though I'm blind, God leads me to priests so that I may make my confession every week. Few blind priests that I know have the same blessing."

"Then I am really glad that I got to speak and share a meal with you. It seems that very few people understand the value of penance the way we do. I find it hard to talk to anyone about it."

"I'll keep you in my prayers, brave knight. May God grant you victory over the evil powers in the world."

Claudius continues forward guided by the copies of maps that he has of the area, which he took from a command center in Rome. The maps show him that there is supposed to be a town guarded by the Church's soldiers in this area, however, all he finds is a ghost town with no signs of life to be seen. Dried blood can be found on some of the buildings along with slashes and places on the stalls and homes that seem to have been hit by a blunt object.

Further in the town, Claudius finds numerous inhuman footprints that suggest that a beastman was recently here. Thunder roars in the distance as it begins to rain.

"Excuse me, sir? What are you looking for?" someone in a cloak says from behind him.

"I'm tracking whatever destroyed this checkpoint. Who are you?" Claudius says.

"Just a friend of one of the people who lived here. My friend forgot something here and I quickly came to pick it back up."

"It's dangerous to be out here alone, especially at night. Where are the knights of the Church?"

"They got orders to move closer to the site of the lower Tower of Blasphemy while the townspeople were ordered to live elsewhere. You should probably leave since you're by yourself as well. It only gets more dangerous from here."

"I know about the dangers, but I didn't know about the soldiers nor the townspeople having to move and I would know about it being from the Aurora family."

"An Aurora?" the stranger says in shock.

"Yes, and I'd like to know who you are and what happened here. There are many signs that this place was attacked particularly by beastmen. Their vampire masters can't be too far from here. In fact, I think there might be one near us."

In the blink of an eye, Claudius takes out his whip and whips the stranger's legs off to reveal that they are a beastman or rather an apeman to be specific.

"You-you would cut a stranger's legs off?"

"Even if you weren't a monster, I'd punish a dishonest man."

"Monster? It's funny you say that-"

Claudius whips near the beastman's face.

"No more nonsense. You will tell me what happened here plainly and simply."

"We were tired of the monsters that were the leaders of the Church and their slaves and decided to do something about them. The serfs from the underground tower gave us that opportunity. Those who accept it were freed while those who didn't were forced to be free, and believe it or not, I was one of the forced, and thank them for doing that. Is that simple enough for you?"

"Yes. I'll allow you a minute to confess your sins to God before I put you out of your misery as a serf."

"There's no need to. I haven't sinned and…I'm …already dead…"

The apeman appears to have died, but he springs to life and screams in pain when Claudius whips the beast's last arm off.

"I'm no fool. I know that beastmen don't die so easily. Be thankful that you have enough pain to offer up as your penance as you slowly die."

Leaving the serf to his slow death, Claudius heads out on his horse to the next nearby checkpoint in the hopes of finding people who haven't turned against the Church but is met by a band of vampires and serfs before he reaches it.

"You killed our messenger? How cruel are-" a vampire says before Claudius whips off their head.

He circles his whip around like a man-made tornado while tearing through every enemy that he comes across. This tactic works until his enemy starts firing arrows at him one of which hits his horse in the head killing it. Using the trees as cover, Claudius runs from the arrows and incoming enemies until he reaches another checkpoint town that is like the last one. Running inside the house and taking shelter, he catches his breath and tries to think of an effective way to kill all the vampires and serfs. The thought of running away doesn't even enter his mind since he thinks that no enemy of the Church should live.

"Hey," a woman whispers as she exits a closet in the room.

In his heightened state, Claudius immediately whips and destroys the closet, but the woman manages to barely dodge his attack. The woman then shows herself clearly in the light with her hood off and arms up.

"Look, look! I'm purely human!" she says.

"How can I be sure of that?" Claudius asks ready to attack again.

"I solemnly swear to God! I didn't accept the serf's offer nor is my body altered in any way! Uh…look if you must."

The woman reveals her body to Claudius who sees that she is clearly normal and then looks away.

"Okay, okay. You can cover yourself," he says.

"I'm sorry. I didn't know how else to convince you."

"Shush. The beasts are approaching."

Going to the window to see what's happening, the two peak outside to see what the beasts and vampires are doing. They begin to search the houses and break into them from below and by jumping into the buildings through the roof.

"If you are a decent man of faith, let's talk and perhaps you can leave us alone," a serf says, "We were forced to work jobs that underpaid us for jobs that worked us to the bone because they said they were protecting us from the inhabitants of an underground tower, but it was those inhabitants who gave us more food and more wealth than what the Church gave us. Those so-called beasts gave us freedom and returned us to the comfortably secluded lives that we had before the Church overexerted her power over us."

"Damned fools," Claudius says as he begins to get up.

"Wait, it's too dangerous to do anything," the woman says while bringing him back down.

Seeing that she's right, Claudius begrudgingly sits back down.

Continuing on, the serf says, "Even those loyal to the Church agree that we're in the right. In fact, most do since we were loyal to her, to begin with. All we ask is that you leave us alone."

The serf motions for the others to come back to him and they follow his orders. To Claudius' surprise, even the vampires retreat back.

"These beasts are telling a half truth," the woman whispers, "They do want to be left alone and the Church did overwork us for very little compensation, but they also-
"

"I don't need to be convinced to act. I'm just looking for an opportunity," Claudius points out.

This opportunity soon comes as the vampires and beasts let down their guard and walk away from the town.

"Why don't you just let them go? We can use this opportunity to escape," the woman says.

"They're evil, sinful creatures that need to face justice and I am their executioner", Claudius says before leaping into action and decapitating several beastmen with one sweep of his whip.

He then goes for the archers killing one after while dodging their arrows. The vampires and beastmen throw themselves at him in an attempt to overwhelm him with numbers, however, Claudius slashes and spins his whip around him in such a dangerous manner that the woman almost gets caught up in it and the fast movements of his whip act almost like an umbrella with holes in it that stops the rain from touching where it goes. Once the last enemy falls, Claudius looks around before exhaling. It is then that another vampire comes out, but this one has three living bodies attached to it. A female's face to the vampire's along with her body while one male body writhes on the vampire's other side and another male resides on the vampire's chest.

"You've killed my friends and those I was trusted to protect," the vampire says.

"So what?" Claudius says as he immediately attacks the vampire.

This hybrid of beastman and vampire is quicker than the others. It dodges every one of Claudius' attacks until it is able to close the distance, cut him twice with his claws, then throw him into the side of a house. Since he is used to pain, Claudius doesn't let it phase him for long and counterattacks as he lets the vampire get close again although it leaps back into the air in fear as his attack is about to land.

"No, no! I won't let you harm them!" the vampire says. It rubs the face of the suffering faces on its body. "This woman is my true love, this on my side is my father, and this on my chest is the first foe I beat in battle. They are all very precious to me. I had to sacrifice an infant to each just so we can be a singular vampire together."

"You're a monster whose blind to their suffering!"

"No, no I'm not! They're alive and they've always supported me in everything I did!" Claudius continues his attack and tries to anticipate the vampire's movements by attacking in places that he expects, and yet, the vampire still dodges his attacks even as he continues to talk. "I combined them with my body then became a vampire so that we can be together forever! You're the heartless monster who won't leave us alone!"

It is then that Claudius thinks of a way to throw the vampire off.

"Did they really agree to combine with you or did you force them?"

"I-I-I it was their decision. Kind of. They said…but I know they always wanted to be with me. They said it themselves!"

"But did they want to be with you in that way? When's the last time you looked at their faces or are you too afraid to look at their horrified expressions?"

"Yes-no-sort of! I-I-I-"

Claudius' words get the vampire to slip up allowing him to wrap his whip around the vampire's throat.

"You're nothing more than a pathetic creature. You're no lover to be treasured, no son to be proud of, and no worthy foe to be conquered."

"St-stop! You're hurting my wife!"

"Cease living already and go to Hell where you won't see the people you claim to love."

To end the fight, Claudius uses all his strength to break the neck of the vampire killing it and freeing the people who were trapped in its body. Though the fight is over and the rain stops, he waits, kneels, and listens for any more possible dangers.

"That was amazing! You killed-woah!" the woman says before again almost being whipped by Claudius. "Stop that!"

"Stop putting yourself in danger."

"We're not in danger anymore. Any other serfs or vampires will probably run away now that you killed the lord of this area."

"That was a lord? It was pathetic."

"It also looks like it beat you up."

"Regardless, I'm surprised the knights here couldn't handle it."

"It's probably because they didn't think to insult him since we knew him from before, but I'm sure you don't want to hear his story."

"It's unimportant and will be forgotten about by God anyway."

"How did you make that whip of yours so powerful? I thought holy and blessed weapons are only effective against vampires."

"That's because this is no ordinary whip. This is the same whip that whipped the back of Christ and has been in my family, the Auroras, for generations. I've made it even stronger by wrapping it around a blessed chain and bits of the cross Christ was crucified on to add to its already awesome power."

"Hold on, so if you're an Aurora then, why are you out here by yourself?"

"My grandfather faced the vampires alone, so I will face them by myself as well."

"Don't you have any backup? You're part of a royal vampire hunting family after all."

"No, though they shouldn't be too far behind me since I told them that I would leave and achieve my God-given purpose. If you see them on your way out of here, you should slow them down."

"What are you talking about? You can't continue on by yourself. Are you crazy?"

"Are you? If they interfere with the will of God, then who knows what calamity could happen because of their sin."

"This insane challenge of facing the vampires by yourself can't possibly be the will of God."

"My grandfather achieved it and he was said to struggle with cowardice. If you think this is crazy, then find the approaching force and get them to move faster. They wouldn't want to miss me prove them wrong."

Claudius walks away in the direction of the tower leaving the woman stunned by his stubbornness and resolve.

Chapter 3 – Results of Lost Hope

After his long travels, Claudius arrives at the site of

the tower to find that an entrance to it jutting out of the

ground is surrounded by beastmen and strange black

skeleton vampires that have little to no skin on their bones

set up in the battle ruined campsite that surrounds the site.

"You are welcome inside," a beastman says.

Despite not being attacked by the beastmen,

Claudius takes advantage of their passivity to kill them

with three large swipes of his whip. He winches after the

attack because of his injury from the vampire lord and remembers what the woman said before offering up the pain the penance and going down the stairs to enter the upside down tower. The stairs down are a crumbled mess with dirt slowly dripping down like an hourglass as if the structure will collapse if broken in the right place. Further down, Claudius enters the first room. This room contains ruined what must've been beautiful statues, paintings, furniture, and more. These ruined objects are being cleaned and fixed by serfs, and just like the beastmen on the surface, these ones don't mind Claudius' presence.

One of them bows to Claudius then says, "Welcome to our castle. Please, do not mind our appearance and make yourself at home. Do you need first aid? We have many doctors that can help you."

The beastman's honest question about his health gives Claudius pause before he stabs it with the end of his whip to silently kill it. This method is the way by which

Claudius slays every single serf and vampire in this castle with a few small fights that end in seconds here and there. Claudius does a thorough cleaning of this castle hoping to find a vampire lord or someone to tell him where the center of the tower is, but he doesn't find any. It then occurs to him that he let his zealotry get to him and did not see the obvious opportunity.

"It wouldn't be a sin to take advantage of their hospitality so I can find the center of the tower," Claudius silently says to himself before realizing another thing. "Guardian angel, my guardian dear. My grandfather's guardian angel led him through his trials to his fate, his wife, and the only serfs who could redeem themselves. Will you not show me the way as well?"

Waiting in silent prayer gives Claudius no answers so he assumes he is where he is meant to be and that his chosen course of action is correct. When he travels further down into the tower, he finds himself in another castle, but this is more like a small town. Every large room contains something different. Some are taverns, bakeries, and restaurants, while others are homes and even churches. To his surprise, the churches practice the same true Catholic faith that he does and there doesn't appear to be any sign of sin or misdeeds, however, he is still uneased by the sight of the beastmen, skeletal vampires, and other vampires who go about their daily business as if they weren't monsters living in a destroyed castle. Reconcentrating his efforts on his task, he goes up to a human serf who is selling clothes that he is making.

Claudius asks him, "Might you know where the lord of this castle is?"

"Dead and in the ground where he belongs. Were you hoping to kill him yourself?" the serf answers.

"I was."

"Well, there's nothing evil in this tower anymore, friend. The serfs have risen up in every castle in this tower, killed the lords, and now we live here in relative peace."

"Relative?"

"Relative because fights will sometimes break out and the Corpus may lose themselves to their sinful ways, but I think we're doing better than one would expect."

"A Corpus? Those creatures of legend are here?"

"You've surely passed several by. There are no true vampires in this area. Not anymore."

"I've been attacked by vampires in this area and my holy whip has killed them."

"If you know the legends, then you know that the Corpus die when God allows them to and when their penance has been paid, so they can enter Heaven. This is a tragedy really. I assume that's why you're all beat up?"

"Yes, and it's why I doubt that the Corpus are here."

"I can't help that and can only assure you that what the Corpus do is outside of their will and they helped us destroy the last of the lords. They even destroyed the blasphemous magic in here that allowed those who used it to teleport."

"I thought Saint Nevar destroyed that when he destroyed the tower."

"He did, but the power to make portals still existed within the tower since it all fell to the ground. Now, thanks to the serfs, that power is forever lost."

"Why did the serfs rebel?"

"Because of Saint Nevar's and Saint Josiah's example. They inspired us to rebel."

"Then why also did the serfs rebel against the Church?"

"We haven't. It's just that we're rebelling against those in Church that take advantage of us and think of serfs as nothing more than irredeemable creatures, which is ironic because of the saints who were serfs and Saint Raven who was a Corpus."

Finding no way to argue with the serf's point, Claudius wonders what to say next for a few seconds.

"Who runs this mess of castles then and how is it still together?"

"The most powerful of serfs that led the assault on the lords. You'll find them a few castles down. As for keeping it together, it probably has to do with the original magic that kept it together and maybe even the will of God since it's so improbable that it's still together."

Hearing that it's God's will that this tower be together ignites Claudius' anger since it sounds like blasphemy to him, but he holds his rage in a way that doesn't show his rage on his face or body language. He then thanks the serf before moving down to visit the leaders of the serfs. On his way there, the two other castles he passes through are filled with similar scenes to the last with one castle having schools and libraries and the second

having farms and bakeries. It is then that Claudius' resolve

wavers as a young child comes up to him and asks him if

he needs a doctor and food since his condition is obvious to

this child. This child is also part wolf, which shows

Claudius that the serfs have been here long enough to

reproduce. In his mind and the mind of some of the others

in the Church, it is an abomination for beastmen to

reproduce despite them still being considered men and

having the same rights as men, assuming the place they're

living in isn't biased against them.

"No, I'm fine," Claudius says to the boy.

The boy doesn't appear to believe him until he says,

"Okay. Hey, how can I look as cool as you? Did you get

that look by being a knight of the Church?"

For some reason, a beastman turns to look at

Claudius at the hearing of this then runs away deeper into

the tower. The beast's suspicious behavior causes Claudius

to chase after it until he finds himself at a dead end that happens to be a graveyard. Many gravestones litter this room with inscriptions that note some of these people as the ones that fought for the serfs' freedom while others are noted as being victims of the vampires and even the Church. Seeing that there's no way out of this room, Claudius feels out the walls and then the graves to try to find a possible hidden exit. The boy being even more curious about Claudius than Claudius is about the beastman follows him into the graveyard to watch him until he becomes impatient and approaches him again.

He says, "What are you looking for, sir?"

"Nothing that should concern you," Claudius answers.

"You look like you're looking for secrets. Let me see if I can help. I found a chicken in a wall once. Don't know why it was there, but I heard the lord that had the castle I found it in loved eating chickens so much that he had to hide his excess stock of it in all sorts of places."

Ignoring what the boy said, Claudius thinks to himself about how to get him to leave.

"Hey, I found a secret staircase! Is this what you're looking for."

The spot where the boy finds the staircase is an ordinary grave that doesn't stick out in any way. Seeing the staircase, Claudius moves passed the boy and down the stairs without even thinking to thank him. This secret reveals an area filled with the mangled bodies of serfs, humans, knights, and other seemingly normal folks. Despite this being a horrid sight, part of Claudius is sourly relieved that his suspicions that this tower still contains evil are correct. Going further in, he finds several beastmen, Corpus, and humans talking to each other.

"The Church has sent their soldiers to kill us! I told you they were going to!" one of them says.

"Maybe this is a misunderstanding. Did you send out your allies to scare them away again? You know that you'll only be met with force and prolong this misunderstanding," another beastman counters.

"That was for a good reason."

"And what reason may that be? So you can continue with these experimentations that you inherited from the lords? I thought that we promised to move beyond this."

"And I thought that you said I can continue them as a last resort because of the knowledge that would be lost."

"That wasn't me. That was my weakened side talking."

"All the Corpus say the same thing, but it's no matter. The lords here had an amazing last resort plan among many and we need to take advantage of it. We can't let their research go to waste."

"Their research that forces people to combine into a singular body? It's an abomination."

"You know how prideful the lords were and how they hated each other. They had a plan to separate themselves once they no longer needed to be combined. Granted, it was in its early stages, but you can see that I've been getting good results in undoing the beast modifications they put on people and those they have combined with others."

"Most aren't well in the mind after your experiments."

"Okay, okay, but it's something that we must make a decision on right now. If I explain any more details of the experiments, then we'll be here all day. The Church's soldiers have already killed the guards on the surface and those in the uppermost castle. Now, after everything that I've explained and the enemy banging at our gates, tell me that you agree with me."

"If the Church sent their soldiers here, then we'd be seeing more than just one and there would be more chaos."

"Tch. You dolt. You don't understand what is happening!"

During this conversation, Claudius is unsure of how to act while listening in on what the enemy knows of him. His enemy is clear and in front of him, however, he is outnumbered and in no shape to take on so many at once, especially with the Corpus among them. The side who is on the side of the Corpus probably wouldn't appreciate it if he killed the beast experimenter even though they are against each other, so that option is out of Claudius' mind. Even so, looking around at all the scientific experimentations done on both the living and dead here that mocks God's creation begs him to act sooner rather than later. Thinking that this was the same challenge that his grandfather faced, Claudius silently prays for bravery, strength, and bravery before leaping into action. He kills several beastmen with an efficient use of his whip and continues to kill multiple of them as he takes advantage of their surprise.

"I told you they're here to kill us!" the experimenter says before working some kind of strange machinery. "I have no choice but to activate it as it is. You can thank me later."

"No, wait!" the Corpus says to no avail.

A dark force comes out of the machine and shakes the very tower. It begins to suck in everything around it and seeing as how it is breaking apart the tower, Claudius assumes that it will destroy it and begins to leave. On his way out, he sees the boy that was following him get sucked in the direction of the dark force. At that moment, it was as if time was moving slowly. Claudius saw the boy's terrified expression and saw him reaching out for him. A part of his soul tugs at him to go save the boy, but he thinks that living the life of a beastman is a curse, so he abandons him.

Even while leaving, Claudius doesn't help anyone who is struggling not to get sucked in or fall victim to the collapsing tower. In fact, he pushes passed them and uses them to pull himself up while they fall. Eventually, Claudius makes his way out of the tower. He falls to the ground out of exhaustion and struggles to even stand. He then watches the staircase that goes into the tower slowly begin to sink down. Part of him remembers the boy and thinks about him again as he feels that he could've saved him.

"No, I couldn't have been able to," Claudius says to the rogue thought in his head.

As the staircase continues to sink, Claudius can see beastmen, Corpus, and other human serfs desperately trying to fit through the narrow hole that none can seem to fit through. The poor people beg Claudius to help them, but he just sits there thinking to himself that they deserve it.

"Pray for mercy because your death is near Repent of your sin of rebelling against the Church," Claudius says to them.

Claudius can hear the people's screams until he hears a loud crushing noise. He lays down before thanking God for his victory and his purpose being fulfilled. After getting up, he limps as he begins his way back home only to be stopped by the ground shaking again.

"I knew it wouldn't be that easy," Claudius says.

Ready for a fight, Claudius takes out his whip, however, when his enemy emerges from the ground where the tower was, he finds that his whip will probably not be enough. What emerges is an enormous beast that is a mile long and the size of a house along with some of the ruins of the tower. It has the body of a wolf, a half wolf, half fly face, the arm of an ape, a claw for another arm, and the wings of two different kinds of insect. The body is split in two by two different mouths and its lower half is that of a snake. Finally, hundreds, if not hundreds of thousands of humanoid figures can be seen writhing around in it appearing to try to break out and faint moans and screams emanating from its body.

"What kind of ungodly abomination are you?" Claudius says.

"We are the result of not leaving us alone and your persecution," the creature says in many voices, "Whereas the Church was uncharitable to us, we have been charitable to you in letting you know this before you die."

"God will not let me fail. To kill you is to achieve my destiny. Guardian angel, grandfather, please grant me strength."

To Claudius' dismay, his whip can hardly do any damage to the beast and is run over and seemingly killed by it soon after. In his half dead state, a light enters his mind to wake it up.

"I'm sorry, grandfather. I've failed you," Claudius says.

"No, you haven't. You still have a chance," Nevar says.

"Is that you, grandfather?"

"I'm here for you, Claudius."

"Hurry and grant me your intercession so I can live up to your legacy."

"You don't have to live up to my legacy in the way that you think."

"What do you think?"

"What do you think I mean? Everyone has their own unique God-given purpose. My father achieved his after he died and I did by being pushed into it by God. You have a different one and I'm sorry to say that it's changed because of your failure, but there's still a chance to make amends."

"What are you talking about? I haven't done anything wrong."

A second light enters his mind, which turns into his guardian angel.

The angel says, "It is true that you were meant to destroy the castle to finally seal away the magic and tainted scientific research within, but you were also meant to save the serfs within and bring them back to the Church and renew their faith in God."

"What? Why couldn't you tell me this before?"

"You were shown it and various people gave you good advice. You were shown the goodness of the serfs, given the advice to ask for help from the vampire hunters in your family's hunting party, and told by a priest that certain people have certain roles in life and not everything harder to do is always right."

"Then leave me to die so I may serve my penance in Purgatory or let me live in pain for as long as God will allow for the same reason."

"That will not be necessary if you do what God actually wills. You have another chance if you follow my son's example who is doing his part correctly," Nevar says.

"My father? If you say so. I won't let you down again, grandfather."

Nevar smiles and then says, "I know you won't, my grandson."

Waking up from his injuries, Claudius finds himself with the other members of his family's hunting party. His wounds are being dressed while others pray over him. They thank God that he's awake, able to stand, and limp around. He makes his way to one of the leaders of the hunting party, or rather, they meet halfway after Claudius says that he wants to see him as his reason for not resting.

"You should be resting, sir," the hunting party leader says.

"I will, but not yet. You must know of the massive abomination out there," Claudius says.

"Oh, we know. It's been out there for three days destroying towns, farms, and attacking cities on a rampage. We already have an army with siege weapons setting a trap for it. It'll be dead before you know it especially since it bit off more than it can chew when it attacked Rome."

"But what you don't know is that it's my fault that the beast is loose."

"We figured you had to do something with it when we found your barely alive body near the ruins of the tower."

"No, I could've stopped it from happening altogether. The beastmen were not allied with the vampires nor was there a single vampire among them. In fact, there were Corpus there. One of them got scared and activated a machine tainted by dark magic that sucked in both the dead and the living to create that creature. What that beastman did is terrible, but it's not like his fears were unfounded as I proved him right by carving a bloody path to him."

"There's no time to worry about that. I'm sure you have some painful penance in mind for yourself to make up for it. I suggest that you don't do it. Do something simpler like praying that rosary the size of your arm for a while and promise God not to ever do something like that again."

"I've already talked to my grandfather and my guardian angel who told me the error of my ways. I told them that I won't let them down."

"Then there's nothing more to say. Let's just keep this between ourselves and not tell anyone. Well, tell no one besides your confessor. We'll get you back to your father soon. I'm sure he hasn't stopped praying for your safety since you left."

Sure enough, when Claudius returns to Rome damaged by the beast he unleashed, his father meets him halfway to hug him. Claudius tells his father what happened in secret and this doesn't change his father's attitude towards him.

"You aren't mad at me?" Claudius asks.

"No, because I know that you'll pick yourself up and become a better man. It was also good to hear that my father said to follow my example despite me being such a klutz. I can already see it in your eyes," his father says.

"I'm…I'm sorry for everything I said about you. About calling you a coward and…for being such a foolish son."

"Don't worry about it. Come, you must get your rest. I'm getting a celebration ready for-Oh! I've spoiled the surprise! I'm sorry!"

"A party? For me?"

"Yes, to celebrate your coming back."

"I…I guess I shouldn't complain or say what is best for myself. I've been doing that for too long and dressing it as God's will. Thank you for everything, father."

Claudius embraces his father and looks forward to the future having learned from his mistakes. Once he gets

Venatores Noctis: Chronicles of a Royal Hunting Family

better, he cleans up his appearance, and even though he is

still a hunter, he vows to do what is right no matter how

hard or easy it may be.

The End

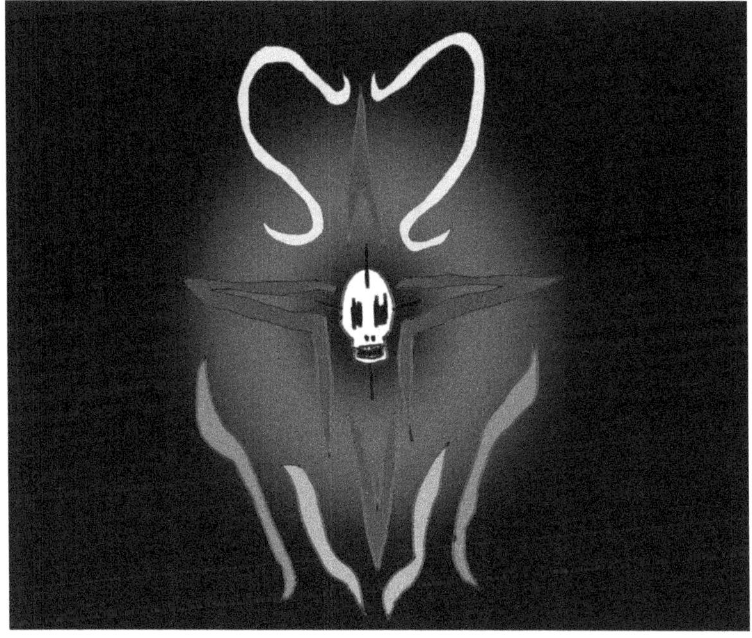

The symbol for the Aurora vampire hunting family inspired

by the crest of Raven Aurora.

Albert Oon

Behind the Story

- Claudius' appearance is inspired by Dante's from the *Dante's Inferno* video game by Visceral Games and EA.

- The Tower of Blasphemy having an upside down part is inspired by how Dracula's castle is flipped upside down in *Castlevania Symphony of the Night*.

- The crosses that you see on the covers of these stories are each the unique crosses of the characters. This is to show the unique cross that each character bears while the quote below it is something that they would say.

- Claudius' cross on his cover was made with Nevar's cross in mind since he is trying to be like his grandfather.

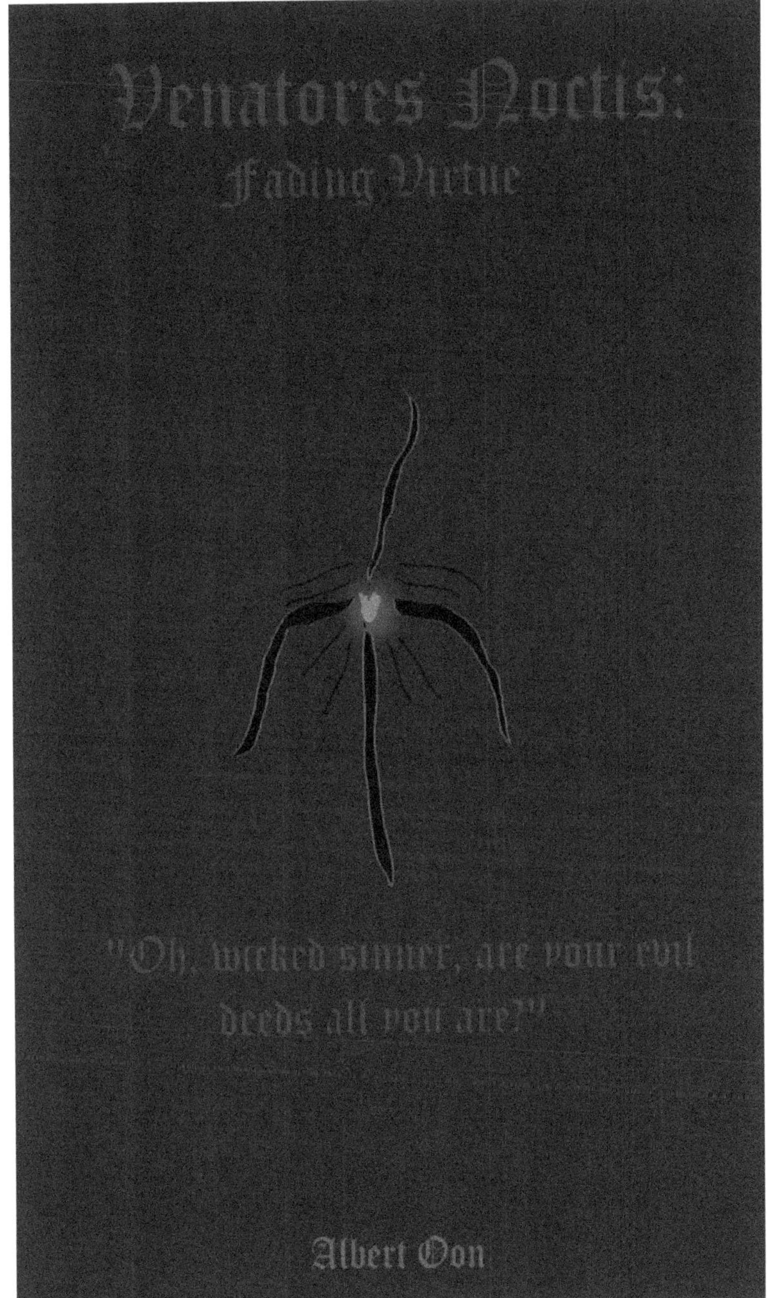
Venatores Noctis:
Fading Virtue
"Oh, wicked sinner, are your evil deeds all you are?"
Albert Oon

Chapter 1 – Using a Spark for an Inferno

Ivy sneaks behind a vampire god and wraps her family's whip around his neck. Despite the metal-like spikes that come from the vampire's neck, go through its face, and come out the top of its head like a crown, Ivy's whip crushes it as if it were paper and makes the god bleed and suffocate.

"It's time for you to die, monster," Ivy says.

"Curses! To think it would end this way," the god says as it struggles to free itself.

"You sealed your fate with your sins!"

"…still…to die at the hands of an Aurora is an honor. Let it be known that I was bested by a hunter from a legendary family-"

The two chuckle before beginning to laugh.

"What? Can't keep up the act anymore?"

"It's one of my favorites, but it does make me laugh. I appreciate the gift of your pleasing pain, Ivy." The vampire god taps out but Ivy doesn't stop strangling him.

"Ivy?"

"What is it? I thought you enjoyed the pain."

"Yes, its way of putting my life in danger is enticing since I rarely ever feel it, but it's sad to say that our good time must end sooner or later. We can continue this again later once I recover."

"Aww, but I'm just getting started."

"Wha-what??

Seeing that Ivy seriously won't release him, the god tries to break the whip around his neck, however, since it is a holy weapon, he only burns his hands as a result. He then uses his vampire god ability to activate the tattoos on Ivy's eye, heart, and the one slightly below her waist. This causes her ecstasy which almost stops her, but she manages to narrowly persevere and behead the god. She then obsessively touches her tattoos as if wanting her curse to continuously feed her pleasure. Her sensations are quieted by another vampire god who enters the room and uses his abilities on her tattoos to calm her down.

"You'll have the chance to experience an even greater pleasure now that you're mine," the god says.

"Don't keep me waiting for long. You know what'll happen if you do," Ivy says before holding the god's arm as if she is his wife.

To show his take over of the city, the serfs of the vampire god hang the decaying body of the god that Ivy killed from the balcony before the new vampire god gives a speech about his take over with Ivy at his side. Those who hear this gather gifts for their new ruler, especially supporters of the old ruler. On the other hand, those who are fearful of this sudden change of rule attempt to leave the city only to be ambushed and killed by supporters of the new rule. Ivy and her master indulge in the pleasures of their take over before going their separate ways to enjoy even more of their spoils given to them by their beastmen serfs.

"Congratulations on another successful takeover, Ivy. How long will you let this new ruler live?" a human woman serf asks.

"Depends how long he can entertain me," Ivy answers.

"What about your other loyalties?"

"Those other gods can wait. The world is already theirs. It's not like there's any rush to replace one ruler with another."

"I mean the Church."

"Rome has long been overthrown and been driven underground so they're no concern of mine. My family hasn't been dedicated to the Church for a few generations now that you mention it. Why do you ask?"

"I heard about the history of your family and thought that part of you would still care for it."

"As far as I know, the God that my family fought for has abandoned us to the darkness in a good way. We can be whoever we want and indulge in every pleasure imaginable until the day we die."

"I wouldn't say that God has abandoned us."

"Have you looked outside at all? The sun never shines. Instead, a warm moon shines during the day and a cold moon shines during the night. This was a blessing given to us by the vampire gods who brought out our true nature through the spell that they call the Eternal Night. You should be enjoying this life rather than worrying about some dying Church and its long lost God. Are you a worshipper of this God? Are you from the Church?"

"Um…I've been in contact with people associated with it. It's how I know what I know."

"Everyone. Leave the room. Except you." Every serf in the room leaves except for the one Ivy is talking to. "You don't belong here, little lamb. Your loyalties are too easy to spot because of the way you talk. I'm sure that even the serfs could tell that you serve the Church. What are you doing here?"

"I wanted to see if it was true that a descendent of the legendary vampire hunting family was under their spell rather than a willing slave, so I snuck my way here to get to you."

"And you would break the curse that's making me a slave to my sin?"

"I was going to try and risk my life so that something would be done about the vampires. Your family has saved the world from them before."

"You're in over your head and out of your mind. I don't need saving, but you do. Leave now before the serfs tell the new ruler of this city that you're here."

"Why would he care that a nobody like me is here?"

"Because you're a native but pure soul. At best, he'll beat you to death with your own limbs and laugh as you scream and cry in agony. At worst, he'll slowly corrupt you and turn you into a mindless serf or a plaything for his desires."

"But your family and you-"

"Have been fighting for the vampire gods ever since the Eternal Night began. I've even been told that my family took part in making it happen."

"I see that there's still light in you since you want to save me. Why won't you fight against the evils of the vampires?"

"What evil? I'm enjoying my life the way it is. Now, no more talking. Get out of here while I distract the god and tell your Church that if they're going to get rid of any evil then they ought to stop giving up priests that baptize the babies the vampires use in their ritual to become the beings that they are."

In a rush, Ivy pushes the woman to a secret exit and throws her out of it. She then runs to find the vampire god who is headed her way.

"I heard there was a servant of God with you. Where is she?" the vampire god says.

"Gone. Why do you have to concern yourself with her when you have me?" Ivy answers.

"Did you get rid of her?"

"I did because I know you'll be giving her all your attention." She kisses and embraces the god. "Give me all you would've given her and more. I crave it. You can even let the serfs watch. Make it a spectacle."

Encouraged by his insatiable lust, the god agrees, tells the serfs that they can be involved, and takes Ivy to the public bedchamber where sex is a show and the serfs involved with it are nothing but playthings whose lives are expendable for the sake of pleasure. There, Ivy tries her best to play around and tease the god for as long as she can while fighting her own desire to give in. This happens for a time until he gets tired of the teasing and uses his abilities on her tattoos to weaken her resistance to the point where she gives in, however, at this same moment, the woman of the Church is brought in by serfs.

"We found her, your majesty!" the serf says as they drag in the woman who is bruised and in chains with her clothes torn.

"Wa-wait! You still haven't satisfied me yet!" Ivy says desperately trying to save the woman.

"Two is better than one since I know you don't like watching."

"Stop it!"

"Oh, but I thought you liked this. Where's your taste for all forms of exquisite pleasure?"

As the god says this, he intensifies Ivy's curse, but she resists it. Flashes of infants dying in blasphemous baptisms and other women and men like her being cruelly killed and degraded fill her mind and ignites a dead part of her that wishes for justice.

For the first time in her life, she prays in her mind, "If you're out there, God who this woman worships, save her. Save her by any means necessary. Pull out a miracle as you are said to do. You can even use me if you wish. Just don't make any more of the innocent die. I beg of you."

At her word, Ivy's hands slowly begin to ignite in flames as she continues to scream while fighting her curse. Everyone in the room watches her in awe before the flames from her hands leap from her hands and spread to everyone and everything until the entire castle they are in catches fire. The god quickly turns to ash whereas the serfs burn to death at various speeds depending on the person's soul. This flame quenches Ivy's lust and wakes her up enough to grab the woman and take her out of the room. Looking out the window, she sees that her flames have enveloped the entire city.

Eventually, the damage done to the castle by her flames is enough to make it collapse, however, a mysterious light envelops them and cuts the falling debris to save them When the dust settles, Ivy and the woman see that the castle has fallen to the ground around them. Every house and building in the city has also fallen and its citizens are all ash. The light that saved Ivy and the woman

Venatores Noctis: Chronicles of a Royal Hunting Family

then manifests as an angel with four wings, four burned arms that hold fire, and a singular eye as a face.

"What kind of god are you?" Ivy asks it.

"I am no god. I am your guardian angel," it says.

"Guardian angel?"

"You can see what the light is manifested as and what it says, and it's your guardian angel?" the woman asks.

"That's what it says."

"Amazing. Every member of the Aurora family was said to be able to see and communicate with their guardian angel. It must be here to lead you to your God-given destiny."

"My what? I don't care for that. I only wanted to save you."

"You wanted more," the angel says, "Your heart yearned for justice and the small piece of your soul that was still pure was allowed to manifest itself as that small flame that burned this entire city and its sinful inhabitants to the ground. Follow the woman's advice and you will be led to the true freedom and justice that you desire."

"I don't desire that. I just want my pleasures-"

"Don't lie and regress back to your old self as you sit on the precipice of change because it will result in your damnation. Follow the woman and burn the world and moon of sin."

With its final word, the angel disappears in a flash of light.

"What did your angel tell you to do?"

"It told me to follow you and burn the world and moon of sin."

"Follow me? It's an honor to be thought of as your guide. I can help you with that, but how are you going to burn the world and moon of sin?"

"No clue. I really don't even know how I used that fire that manifested from my soul."

"I see. We'll figure it out. You still have your

family's whip with you, right?"

"I still got it."

"Then we'll be good for now. Follow me."

"As if I have a better choice."

Ivy follows the injured woman unsure of the future

ahead of her but somehow feeling freer than ever before.

Chapter 2 – New Purpose and People

As both Ivy and the woman walk through the city, Ivy hears the faint sound of crying infants.

"Do you hear crying infants?" Ivy asks.

"It's faint. Do you think…" the woman says.

At the thought of the implication, Ivy runs to the source of the noise and hastily removes the rubble muffling it. She finds crying infants wrapped in the same light that her guardian angel had. Her heart flutters in joy while holding as many infants as she can and trying not to cry.

"Thanks be to God. It's a miracle," the woman says.

"It's a miracle they haven't been killed while their serf mothers and fathers did. This place used to be a place where infants were born for the sake of them being used as sacrifices or experimented on to later become serfs. Wait, if the infants here are okay, then the rest must be," Ivy says.

People with cloaks and weapons approach the two with caution.

Ivy takes her whip out and then says, "Who are you?"

"Bernice?" a man says.

The man takes off his hood to reveal himself as someone that the woman recognizes. Seeing him causes Bernice to run and hug him.

"I'm so glad that you're safe," Bernice says to the man.

"And I am even more glad that you're alive. It's a miracle that you didn't die or were enslaved when you went on your suicide mission."

"How did you survive the city catching on fire and what are you doing out here?"

"The flames didn't affect us even though they spread beneath the city and we're here to see what happened and if it's actually safe to live above ground. Since these infants are alive, I'm sure the others are saving the rest from the burned down facilities that produced them. How did you survive?"

"The flames didn't affect us either and this Aurora's guardian angel saved us from a collapsing castle. She also started the fire with her hands believe it or not."

"Did she really?"

"I don't even understand how I did it and the angel says that I'm supposed to burn the world and moon of sin. It's ridiculous."

"Well, if you wanted to save me and save these infants, then there must be a part of you that still yearns for justice and truth."

"I didn't want to see another person be corrupted against their will in front of me. I also can't stand the sacrifice of infants, especially because-no, forget it."

"Okay. Whatever the case is, we should get these infants to safety."

"Right."

With the man and his friend's help, Bernice and Ivy take the infants down below the city where there are many like them. In this underground part of the city lies the Church of God. Many parts of it are decorated with crucifixes, statues of saints, images of the Blessed Mother, and other holy images.

"It's a wonder that this place was never discovered," Ivy says.

"That's because the holy images we have here dull the senses of the vampires and gods and because our God protects us," Bernice says.

"If you say so. I've seen plenty of your own captured, tortured, defiled, and maimed despite their constant pleading for their God's help."

"But God did answer my prayers and deliver me from the vampires and showed me His purpose for you. It's true that God doesn't seem to answer all our prayers, but that's for a good reason beyond our understanding."

"It's the Aurora," a citizen of the underground Church says.

"Isn't their family traitorous?"

"They were traitorous to begin with even after they were considered heroes."

"They even still use the whip that one of their ancestors used to whip the back of Christ as if it's some honorable weapon."

"Those legends about them saving our world are false."

"Ignore them," Bernice says.

"I know that. Where are you taking me anyway? Is your pope here?"

"No. I don't even know if we have a current one. I'm taking you to a mystic who might be able to tell you how to fulfill God's will for you."

Even though she doesn't know what a mystic is, Ivy lets herself be led to one that Bernice knows of. When she meets the mystic, she becomes even warier of him because of the man's blindness. The mystic gets up as soon as Ivy enters the room and somehow walks in front of her despite his blindness.

"You're Ivy Aurora. It's an honor to meet you," the man says.

"How did you know that? How can you even see?" Ivy says.

"I may not be able to see the physical reality, but my spiritual sight is second only to my fellow mystics. Give me your hands so that I may tell you what you want to know."

Ivy allows the man to touch her hands out of curiosity.

"What do you see, blind man?"

"I can see a faint ember that is struggling to stay alive. This is the last thing keeping your soul alive that yearns to burn for justice."

"It yearns to burn? Haha, something in my soul telling you what it wants to do is the most absurd thing I've heard today when I know it better than you do and there's nothing in me that says that."

"Oh, but it does. You just silence it even as it whispers to you, and because of what happened, it's a whisper that you can no longer ignore. The ember was ignited when you saw innocent people tortured, die, and become corrupted."

"That did make me upset, but-"

"But where you really wanted God, truth, and justice to be real was when you heard and witnessed the death of baptized infants especially the death of your child."

Everyone who hears it looks at the mystic and Ivy.

"How do you know about my child?!"

"Your soul told me about it."

"Well, it won't tell you anything else!" Ivy tries to move away, but she feels that she's paralyzed in place and can only move her shoulders. Her eyes then focus on her guardian angel who appears in her sight without warning and shows her that it is the one that is holding her. "What did you do to me?"

"I'm not doing anything. It's your angel who wants you to realize your true nature so that you will repent and save your soul."

"Why now when it's let me be who I am? Why now when God let the vampires take over the world and enact their will on everyone?"

"I cannot say for sure. Perhaps we deserved it. Perhaps it is necessary so that a greater good might be born from it. The only thing that I can say for certain is that you are the one who will save us with your fire."

"People keep saying I should use it, but I don't even know how to!"

"You have an idea of how. Do the same thing as you did before. Give yourself over to God and you will be complete and who you are meant to be. Here, I will allow you to feel the same peace that you felt when God touched your soul and allowed your flames of righteous anger the ability to manifest."

"I didn't feel any peace…"

It is then that Ivy remembers the touch of God that happened for less than a second. This feeling is like that of resting after a day of work when everything is done or something close to the feeling of being in Heaven or even closer to the feeling of true love.

"There it is. Remember that feeling and you will truly become the Ivy Aurora that God made you to be. Forget it, and you will become like the vampire gods. Nothing but an empty vessel for demons."

With that said, the mystic lets go of Ivy's hands. She loses the feeling of peace and is back to feeling empty and craving physical pleasures, which she begins to hate. Ivy then leaves the mystic and goes to Bernice.

"That was amazing what the mystic told you. Now you know how to fulfill your God-given role," Bernice excitingly says.

"Uh huh," Ivy lukewarmly responds.

"I'm sorry about your child. If you need anyone to talk to-"

"I don't want to talk about it to anyone."

"Okay, okay."

Before they have a chance to relax, they see that the people are beginning to pack up. Concerned about this, Bernice goes to one of the Church leaders to ask why this is.

"Most of us are afraid that the vampires that come here will annihilate us because of what they'll find. Because of this, we've decided to move to another place," the leader says.

"Why's that? God has given us Constantinople to be our own?" Bernice says.

"It makes sense," Ivy comments, "This city isn't yours just because your God burned it and made it safe for you. The gods may just bring in an army to destroy you or worse when they learn of what happened, which I'm sure they already have."

"And just because an Aurora is helping us doesn't mean that this one will save the world now. Don't get me wrong. I appreciate your help and trust that God has good things for us. I just don't trust you too well because of what your family has done as of late."

"Then this is where we part ways."

"Hold on. I still know of your skills that we can put to use."

"I don't think holy people like you want my skills."

"You know what I'm talking about. Your skills as a fighter and not a prostitute. We'll pay you to keep us safe until we find a place we can live. It's been decided by the council that you can have any reward for this within reason."

"Oh? Why's this?"

"We do not forget the good that your family has done and what you have done according to Bernice. The Auroras did stay faithful to the Church until the generations of Saint Claudius' blessed children and grandchildren passed away."

"I see. I accept."

"Sir, I think we should do more than just pay her. She has the blessing from God to change the world," Bernice says.

"If it comes to that, then by all means she can stay with us permanently. It's just not something that we see happening in the near future."

"Ivy…"

"Don't worry about me, Bernice. I'll be fine. Now, come on, and let's help your people pack up. The gods will be on their way here before you know it."

Bernice reluctantly accepts the reality of the situation and silently prays that Ivy stays with them. After packing up, the followers of God and Ivy load as much as they can on the horses and handmade carriages the Church has kept fed and hidden in the underground before heading out. Ivy sits on the rear carriage while other defenders sit on the outside carriages with their blessed weapons drawn and ready for a fight. It isn't long before they get this fight as many beastmen and vampires come running their way. The defenders hardly manage to defend the carriages besides Ivy who can narrowly hold her own.

"Ivy!" Bernice says who is under attack.

"Come on, come on! Don't you want to save your worshippers, God?" Ivy silently thinks.

She tries to remember the feeling to activate her flames until she starts to pray for a second, which lights up her whip. Her whip is also extended and able to release fire projectiles out at distant enemies that she uses to save Bernice and the other carriages.

"I knew you could do it!" Bernice says.

"Oh, please. I don't even know what I did," Ivy says.

Many more enemies approach them until not even Ivy's upgraded whip cannot help them.

"Come on! Where's that feeling?" Ivy thinks to herself.

Soon after, Bernice and those around her are overwhelmed and their horses are killed so that the carriages crash. This causes Ivy to panic to try to strengthen her flames.

"Come on, flames, activate already! You've already allowed so many innocents to die!"

"Watch out!" Ivy's carriage driver says.

A group of beastmen and vampire serfs throw themselves at their carriage causing it to crash.

"You have to do something now or we're all going to die or worse. Do what you did before," Ivy silently says to God.

At her allowing God to act through her, Ivy's strength is restored. She becomes like a fiery tornado that tears through the army until the gods activate her curse to bring her down. Ivy is able to resist her temptations only for a short while until she is consumed by them.

"Where's that feeling? I can't find it," Ivy says to herself while trying to resist her curse.

The flames from her whip are gone along with her strength. Many of the worshippers of God are killed while few are cursed with the fate of whatever twisted desire the gods have for them.

"So, this is the famous Aurora. It appears that there's more to her than her sexual proficiency and strength in battle," one of the gods says as they approach her.

"I think we have our explanation as to how Constantinople burned down," another says, "I say we don't kill her and use her as a weapon to dominate the other gods."

"I say we should. Her family and she have done great services for my family and friends in more than one way," a third god says.

"You don't think she'll turn on us?"

"People like her, like us, only need to be satiated with pleasures of all kinds. Just look how happy she is now."

"Oh, that's right, but for now, let's get her back to our castles. Let her pleasures overwhelm her until she falls unconscious. I don't want to take any chances after what she did, but I also want her to have a taste of her future reward for serving us."

"You are too generous, but I do want to see her lose herself in an overwhelming amount of pleasure. Let me see it!"

The pleasure inflicted on Ivy through her curse is increased until she falls unconscious. She is then taken with the rest of the worshippers of God to the combined castle of these vampire gods and a new horror that awaits them.

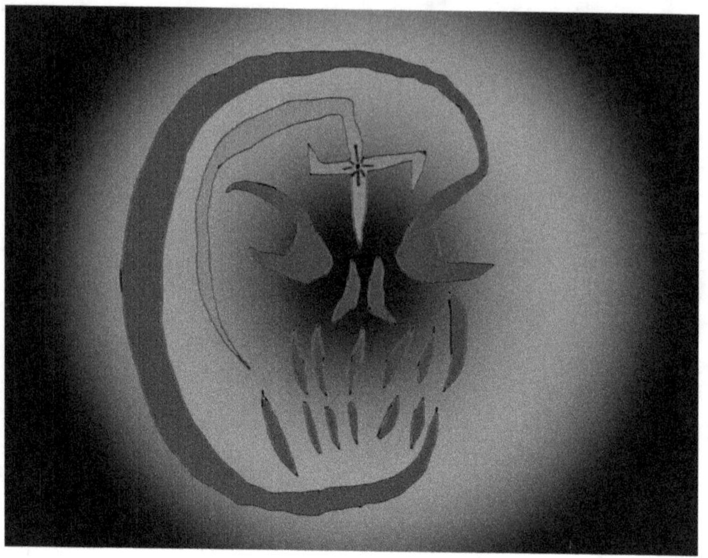

Chapter 3 – Burn the Curse, Burn the Moon

To her surprise, Ivy awakens unchained in a rather luxurious room. She finds that her whip isn't by her side and that nothing has been done to her. Her wounds from her fall have even been healed. Part of her is thankful that she doesn't have to help the worshippers of God anymore, but at the same time, she feels worried about them being corrupted, especially Bernice. To see where she is, Ivy looks out the window to see that she is in a castle with neighboring castles around it and smaller buildings around them that are puny in comparison. Her curiosity about Bernice and the others then moves her to exit the room.

In contrast to her luxurious room, Ivy finds herself in a hallway full of cells where people are being corrupted and tortured. Her want for justice slowly begins to burn as she sees this and finds herself unable to do anything. Going further along, she finds a room where a person is becoming a vampire god. This person smashes several holy objects until they are cursed with the blasphemous baptism and covered with the blood of a baptized infant. Black spikes come out of the new god's neck, go through its face, and emerge at the top of its head as if crowning it. Seeing the infant die a gruesome death and the other lords and gods celebrate it forces Ivy to act even though she is easily seen by the gods who wished her to see this.

"Ah, we were just going to wake you up and bring you here. You will be a god like us. Isn't this a grand blessing?" one of the gods says.

"Why? It's not something that I want," Ivy says.

"Because of your power and because of your sinful soul. A person can only become a god like us if most of the light of God is lost from a person's soul and yours is perfect."

"I can't use that power without asking God for it."

The gods look at each other and consult one another. Even the new god has a say in this.

One of them speaks for the rest as it says, "That will be of no issue. With you allied with us, God will no longer be able to use you against us. As a god, you'll live eternally blaspheming God with every action, every breath of your life. You will have true freedom to do whatever you want."

"I don't care for God, but I don't want this! Above all, I don't want an innocent infant to die for my sake."

"You don't have a choice in this. Besides, we can see from your sinful soul that you would like nothing different than the pleasures that only sin can afford, or do we need to remind you?"

"I think we do," a god interrupts, "I think we should have her pleasure herself with the body of the holy woman."

"The what?"

"One of the women who was with you was a fine treat indeed. She prayed out loud for her God and you to save her. Here, we have no more use of her corpse."

The god throws over to Ivy the mangled body of Bernice who is barely recognizable to her. Ivy looks at her face in horror and begins to sob as she silently apologizes to her.

"That woman was something else. If there was anyone holy among that herd of sheep, it was her because of how strongly she resisted us until her death. Having our way with her was some of the best fun I had in months."

"I'll kill you!" Ivy says with her fists raised.

"With what? Your bare hands? Your nonexistent fire powers or perhaps this?" the god says before showing Ivy her whip and crushing it with its hands. "You have nothing to fight us with. Perhaps you'll find something later."

"We would like a good challenge since the Church of God doesn't give us any."

"It would be nice, but for now since you're so resistant, we should get you to relax. Perhaps sin a bit more before you become a god so that you'll become more powerful."

"Maybe we should actually have her pleasure herself with that corpse. Oh, what beautiful corruption will be born from that!"

"Perhaps we should."

The gods activate Ivy's curse and put it into overdrive.

"I'm sorry, Bernice," Ivy says to herself.

"Get up. You can still fight this," a voice says in her head.

Inside her mind, Ivy sees her guardian angel.

"I can't do anything."

"You can allow God to act through you."

"But I can't. The only thing that I can feel like I can do is to give myself over to my sins."

"I felt totally out of control of myself too once, but submission to God is true freedom," an unfamiliar voice says to her.

"I was afraid of the destiny God put me in. Still, I trusted in Him and triumphed with the help of my friends," another voice says.

"I let my pride and zeal overcome me, and yet, God gave me a second chance," yet another voice chimes in along with many others who give their testimony of service to God.

"Who are these people?" Ivy asks her angel.

"These are your saintly ancestors. They are praying that you overcome your challenges and are giving you the opportunity to do so. The choice is up to you."

"Why does it have to be me? I'm nothing but a worthless whore."

"You are not that to God. You are His precious creation that He died for and even now, He wants you to live and redeem yourself."

Touched by this, Ivy's strength begins to restore itself.

"I know you can do it, Ivy!" the voice of Bernice says from beyond.

Hearing the voice of Bernice and finally beginning to understand her purpose in life, Ivy prays to God, "I see now or at least see as best I can. Okay, God. Do with me what You will. Let the flames of justice burn through me and put an end to this eternal night."

At her word, Ivy and everything and everyone around her begins to catch fire. This fire spread from not only this castle and the surrounding castle but quickly spreads throughout every inch of the world to burn the evil from it. Cities and long lasting monuments easily crumble while the vampires and their serfs of all kinds burn to ash as well. While this is happening, Ivy is struggling to keep this fire alight as it burns her as well. Despite the pain, she holds on preferring the freeing pains of the divine fire over the dark pleasures of her curse being inflicted on her by demons. Her angel, her ancestors, and Bernice continue to strengthen her with their prayers to keep her going.

Eventually, the castle around her crumbles, but her angel protects her from this. The entire world burns until finally, a flare shoots out from it to blow up the false moon to bits. After a short while, Ivy's fire subsides and the world is free from the slaves of sin and false gods. Looking around, Ivy sees the ruins of the castle around her. Not many survived with her in this location with all of them saying that a light protected them, a light that Ivy explains to them was their guardian angel.

The smoke from the flames then dissipates to reveal the sun's light that hasn't shined on the earth for generations. It is then that Ivy realizes that the curse marks on her are gone and that she feels freer than ever.

She then gets down on her knees and says, "Thank you, God, for being so patient with me! I promise you that the sinful woman that I was burned up and the woman that you want me to be has emerged from her ashes. Please, continue to grant us your aid and help us rebuild a better society in Your name."

Ivy takes a couple of the infants that survived, kisses them, and leads the survivors of the fire to a better tomorrow as she follows the light of God that now lives within her.

The End

𝕭𝖊𝖍𝖎𝖓𝖉 𝖙𝖍𝖊 𝕾𝖙𝖔𝖗𝖞

- Ivy blowing up the moon is inspired by Zangetsu cutting the moon in half in the *Bloodstained Curse of the Moon 2*'s secret ending.

- Ivy's appearance is inspired by Lisa's from *Genshin Impact*.

- The moon that you see in chapter 3's chapter image is a symbol of the Eternal Night and the cross is made to look strange on it since what is right in the world is made to seem strange and foreign in the eyes of everyone in it.

- I didn't know what to call Bernice until the name entered my head. When I looked it up, it turns out that Bernice means "bringer of victory". Because of this, I thought the name fit perfectly since she is the reason why Ivy is able to bring God's victory over evil.

- Ivy, on the other hand, was named so because she

gave me *Poison Ivy* from the DC comics vibes.

When I looked up what the name Ivy meant, then I

decided to use it since it means "God's gift".

Venatores Noctis: Chronicles of a Royal Hunting Family

If you liked these stories, then give these others a try!

Evil can only prosper if good men refuse to do the right thing.

Alessio is a normal high school student who can see the spiritual

and ends up becoming an exorcist. Across this series, he'll learn

the consequences of eternity and that the worse enemy is not

only from within but also those in our Church and even our

family. If we and those around us don't fulfill our

responsibilities, then how can we expect the world to change?

My God, my God, why hast thou forsaken me?

Even if you try to be faithful to God and pray for help, you'll still find yourself falling into sin every now and then. These dark fairy tales set in a rotting world that is washed by blood then blessed by fire tell the tales of people who are trying to be faithful and despair in their imperfection, but find that even in this, they find that they are still loved and mercy is always available to those who ask for it with pure intentions.

Flames darken and sinners become saints in this series of dark fantasy short stories. From violent murderers to self-proclaimed gods, these short stories follow people with muddy pasts where salvation seems to be out of reach as they make their way to the path of repentance.

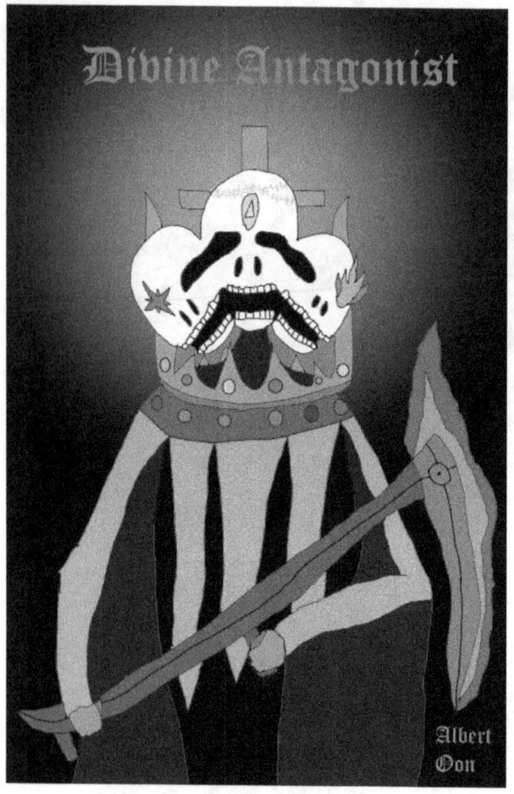

No one, but God knows what is best for us and our world. In these stories where God almost seems to be the antagonist, the world either chooses prosperity and comfort at the cost of sin and man-made gods or truth at the cost of suffering God instructs various people to do His Will while the Deceiver tries to pull them in the other direction. What happens is a result of man either doing the right thing and following God or doing evil and falling to ruin.

Venatores Noctis: Chronicles of a Royal Hunting Family

Check out my free eBooks on Smashwords as well!

A mysterious group of attackers destroy Zain's tribe and leave him as the only survivor. In his agony, an angel comes to him, resurrects his tribe as an army of the undead, and tells him to destroy the people that killed the people he loved. He does this only to be hated and labeled as a criminal by the rest of the tribes. Despite this, he strives to free the rest of the tribes from corruption.

In a world where demons physically manifest themselves through people, Astra and a band of exorcists have captured Estella, a woman heavily possessed by demons. Estella is being transported to a place to be freed from the demon's possession and to remember who she was, but an ambush forces Astra and Estella to endure each other as they try to get Estella the help she needs. Along the way, they'll learn who Estella was and about each other and what is keeping them from being good and saintly.

Dracula and his army are conquering a weak Europe with more demonic forces infesting the East. Alucard, Dracula's son, and his wife Silvia are also vampires, but they're going to destroy Dracula in order to save the world. Even though they will die along with the rest of the vampires, undead, and demons, they go anyway despite the consequences and the many challenges they will face.

To be a gluttonous sinner means to have physical and worldly powers that no normal human can have, but it also means that you'll never be satisfied enough. Lilith is bitten and becomes one of these sinners against her will and must choose to either fight to stay human or give in and slowly become a monstrous sinner until no part of her humanity remains.

Check out my blog, Albert Oon: Behind the Stories, for free short stories, free book samples, song/poem attempts, and more! Follow me on Twitter, Facebook, Instagram, and LinkedIn to see what I'm doing next.